Songlines

A Novel

John Graham-Pole

HARP Publishing

The People's Press

Clydesdale, Nova Scotia

Canada

HARP The People's Press

216 Clydesdale Road

Clydesdale, Nova Scotia

Canada, B2G 2K9

www.harppublishing.ca

email: harppeoplespress@gmail.com

tel# 902.863.0396

Catalogue-in-Publication data is on file with Library and Archives Canada

ISBN: 978-1-990137-12-9

Cover art: "Caritas" - Gillian McCulloch

Graphic design: Cathy Lin

The Circle of Abundance Indigenous Program, Coady International Institute, St. Francis Xavier University: https://coady.stfx.ca/circle-of-abundance;and David Suzuki Foundation (one nature): https://davidsuzuki.org receive 20% of all sales, distributed equally.

Proudly Supporting
DAVID SUZUKI FOUNDATION
davidsuzuki.org

Fier De Soutenir
FONDATION DAVID SUZUKI
fr.davidsuzuki.org

COADY
INTERNATIONAL INSTITUTE
ST. FRANCIS XAVIER UNIVERSITY

Praise for Songlines

Songlines is a beautiful love story about a young couple grappling with fatal brain cancer. Written from the perspective of a student who is considering going to medical school and how living life on the other side of the stethoscope changed her perspective on care giving. This is a story of bravery and heart. Dr. John Graham-Pole channels his decades of experience working with young people with cancer to spin a truly lovely tale about living life with meaning, and what it means to love and care for someone at the time of their greatest need.

William Slayton, MD, Professor and Chief,
Pediatric Hematology-Oncology, University of Florida

Songlines is a poignant, tough love story of courage, determination, and nobility of character.

Sheldon Currie, PhD, Author,
Down the Coaltown Road, The Glace Bay Miners' Museum

Reading *Songlines* brought me to tears—some of sadness, many of joy. A beautiful, compelling story with deep authenticity, coming from someone with many years of lovingly caring for others.

Judy Rollins, PhD, RN, Department of Family Medicine and
Pediatrics, Georgetown School of Medicine

This sensitively crafted novel is written by a beloved oncologist who understands more about his patients than could be learned from an MRI scan. Difficult issues— lesbian parents, gender roles, use of morphine and cannabis, how to present bad news—are all covered. The treatment of the couple's intimate life is sensual and beautiful. Dr Graham-Pole knows that love is possible on the cancer journey, that it can grow in pleasure, worth, intimacy and dignity.

Rebecca Brown, M.Div., Spiritual Care and Death Educational Counselor; Creator and Founder of *Streetlight*, University of Florida

When was the last time you witnessed the magic of listening to music that reminded you of your own heartfelt story? With notes of deep love, professional caring, compassion, expertise, and hope, *Songlines* struck my own personal and professional chords. Serving as a powerful reminder that along the tracks in the journey of cancer, when the patient is held truly at the centre of care, a beautiful story can unfold. *Songlines* is that story.

Barbara Farquharson Fry, BN, MAdEd. Author*,*
Fast Facts for the Clinical Nurse Manager

Dr. Graham-Pole blends his vast experience as a pediatric oncologist and his appreciation of the value of the arts in health together beautifully in this touching novel. It makes me want to start a chorus at my hospital!

Alan Siegel, MD, Wellness Director,
National Organization for Arts in Health

I had a personal visceral reaction to reading *Songlines*, having walked the walk with a teenage family member who struggled through 15 years of cancer. This novel skillfully addresses what happens when a young adult is brought to his knees by cancer, as are those around him. Is this a depressing book? No, not at all. There is music, poetry, humour, profound compassion, profound learning—all find a role in this story.

Zané deNoncourt, Schoolteacher

Songlines takes the reader through the sublime setting of a university choir to the mysteries of cancer, focusing on the healing power of music. It is reminiscent of my graduate research at University of Florida where I saw first-hand the power of music in healing in the oncology unit.

David Akombo, PhD, Dean, Faculty of Culture, Creative and
Performing Arts, University of the West Indies

I connected with this very moving and relatable story in so many ways.

Marjorie Bowman, RN, MScN, Advanced Practice Nurse,
The Ottawa Hospital

This beautiful book is about music, medicine, and loving care. There is optimism and levity, despair and courage, a deepening love between Jonah and Ellen as they interact with both standard and natural healthcare. The last words of the book make powerful meaning as Ellen considers her next steps: *Every act of care I could offer to another would be an offering of love for my beloved Jonah. And an act of healing for myself.*

As a career nurse, I would recommend this book to all patients and families I have cared for, physicians I have interacted with, and nurses engaged in loving care everywhere.

love Barb.

Barbara Heatley-O'Neil, RN, BScN, MAdEd.
Certified Professional Co-Active Coach

Also by John Graham-Pole

Non-Hodgkin's Lymphoma (Editor and co-author)

Illness and the Art of Creative Self-Expression

Physical

On Wings of Spirit (Editor and co-author)

Quick: A Pediatrician's Illustrated Poetry

The Arts and Health (Co-authored)

Journeys with a Thousand Heroes: A Child Oncologist's Journey

The People's Photo Album (Co-authored)

Blood Work

A Boy and His Soul

Dedication

For Rebecca Brown, creator of <u>Streetlight</u>, a palliative care prgram engaging hundreds of college students in helping hospitalized youth through the "valley of the shadow of death"

Note to the Reader

This is the third book in my trilogy of novels inspired by caring for children with cancer and their families. Although I have set this story in two Canadian universities, it is a work of fiction based on my real-life experience at an American university.

The events I write about may be distressing to those who have encountered cancer—either themselves or in a loved one—but I hope they will find it uplifting too.

One

September

Joy fills me every Friday morning, no matter what kind of day I've had—or week for that matter. Friday mornings are when my boyfriend, Jonah, and I and six other friends gather for choir practice. Our choir director, Raig—short for Moraig though no one ever calls her that—makes sure she picks songs that have us singing our hearts out. I love how our voices have come to blend and harmonize.

"Okay, let's switch things up," Raig says. "I'm after a different mix of voices. One soprano on each end—Ellen, Therese." She blesses us all with her big broad smile as she calls out our new placements. "Then Dawn, you right in the middle, with Vern and Jonah on either side of you. And you two altos—Amy, Carole—right next to them. Space yourselves out, there's plenty of room."

We giggle as we jostle into our new positions. Dawn, the one music major among us, sings most of the solos, so putting her front and centre makes sense. And at five foot nine, she's not dwarfed by Jonah our tenor or Vern our bass on each side of her. The features of Dawn's face are strong and beautiful, and she likes to pile her tight black curls high over her head. Her voice has the power and range of a gospel singer—something I could never approach. Though I'm proud of the high notes I can reach, and it's gratifying how smoothly my voice blends with my roommate and best friend Therese's.

Vern rooms with Jonah and Bill, the choir's guitar player, and has been dating Therese since eleventh grade. He has a freewheeling style with a lot of energy, which seems to suit Therese, who is very much the quiet and thoughtful type. Vern, Therese, and I are all biology majors, so we're a pretty close gang. I haven't got to know the altos, Amy and Carole, too well as they're new to the choir this year. They're both in second year, while Vern and Bill are third years and Jonah and Therese and I are all in our final year here at Ramsay. Amy dyes her hair different colours—today it's lilac with a few darker highlights—and she wears a nose ring. She's quiet and hard to read. Carole is much more emotional and seems down a lot of the time. She's rake thin, and I can't help wondering if she has an eating disorder. Their two low-pitched voices combine nicely, and both of them have shared with us how these choir sessions lift their spirits.

And me? I'm Ellen Grace Mackie, and I'm a biology major. I like to think of myself as a pre-med, because I've set my heart on making it into medical school next year. If I can keep my grades up in the A-plus, A-minus range, if I score high marks on the MCAT, if I can get strong reference letters from my profs, if I can score an interview…if, if, if. I'm five foot eight, healthy-looking, and not blessed—or cursed—with film star looks. Jeans and a crop top suit me better than a backless mini-dress, and doing my curls up usually means twisting them into a messy bun.

"Okay, let's try an old favourite to get you warmed up," Raig says as we settle ourselves into our new arrangement. "See how repositioning you like this works out. Vern, Jonah, don't drown out the altos. You all set, Dawn?"

Bill, the eighth member of our choir, takes up his spot close to Raig in front of the rest of us, hefts the strap of his Yamaha acoustic guitar over his shoulder, and strums the opening chords of Leonard Cohen's "Hallelujah." At six-foot three or four, he towers over Raig and handles his guitar like it's a toy. He's older than the rest of us, maybe twenty-four, and his blond thatch of hair is already receding.

I feel shivers move through my spine as we hum the background harmony to Dawn's solo voice. I let my feelings pour out, happy the tickle in my throat isn't marring my pitch. Our eight voices rise in unison in the final refrain of Cohen's paean of pain and celebration.

This basement room in the old health centre stands a good fifty metres distant from the main hospital, but Raig still worries some authority figure will burst in to complain about the noise. Worse still, demand to know who the blankety-blank has given us the okay to even be in here. When I asked her how she'd found the room, Raig said, "I simply went on the hunt around the whole medical centre complex when I first got the idea of forming the choir. And here was this nice empty room that looked like it hadn't been used in a dog's age. Squatters' rights, I decided."

As the echoes of the last hallelujah resound off the ceiling, we give ourselves a round of applause, shed a few group tears, then laugh and move on to Joel Plaskett's "Love This Town," followed by Raig's arrangement of "Farewell to Nova Scotia." And just like every Friday morning I feel the rapture of singing in harmony with my friends and fellow students.

I'm the only choir member not from the Maritimes; most of them have grown up on these melodies. My hometown is Gananoque, less than thirty clicks east of Kingston, Ontario, and I'm an only child. But Nana Jackson, my mom's mom, was from Yarmouth on Nova Scotia's South Shore, so Mom and Dad thought it was cool that I wanted to come here for university. It was she who turned me on to the idea of medical school.

Nana had Parkinson's, and she knew everything there was to know about it. That summer before starting university I spent a lot of my time with her. Taking her for walks, going with her to medical appointments, cooking up new recipes together, helping her with jigsaws as her sight deteriorated, and reading to her when she couldn't sleep. We even took up dancing together to music from her old CD player, after we both learned how much it could help with her balance and agility. Despite her physical frailty, she never lost her sharp mind, and she loved it that I wanted to learn all about the latest research and the new treatments for her horrid illness.

The choir members have gotten into the habit of lingering after our weekly rehearsals. To hang out together, talk about our lives and about the hospital patients we've become buddies with. Raig told each of us when we joined the choir that becoming patient buddies was essential to membership.

"Lots of patients have very few visitors, other than immediate family and the doctors and nurses," she'd pointed out. "And almost all the conversations focus on their illness. Their awful symptoms and their mostly awful treatments. What every patient needs is someone to hang out with who isn't the bearer of bad news. Or isn't going to cart them off for yet another X-ray or painful procedure. The deal is, I'll introduce each of you to a couple of patients, and you get to spend time with them. A lot of them will be children and teens but by no means all. I'll make sure you get to meet some oldies too."

"That sounds great," Dawn had said. "A bit like the artists' program I was part of last year. We were there to make art with the patients. But the big thing was to be a new friend to hang out with when every hospital day was the same old, same old."

When Raig started the choir last year, it didn't have a name. "What do we call ourselves?" I'd asked.

"Great question," Raig responded. "Let's brainstorm!"

"How about The Buddies," Vern suggested. "Or The Minstrels?"

"I think that's been taken," Bill said. "How about Good Neighbours?"

"I think we need something that really describes what we're all about," Raig said. "That we're not only here to support patients, but that we're also a choir."

"I get a great music magazine called *Songlines*," said Dawn. "The latest songs, the scoop about new bands, stuff like that."

"I like that name," Jonah said. "I learned about songlines in one of my anthropology classes. It's what the Indigenous Australians named the tracks across the land they believed their creators made—crisscrossing the whole continent. They said their ancestors left them during Dreamtime as geographic routes but also as sacred rituals."

"You told me they were ceremonial places, right?" I added.

"Right. And they told stories as they wandered and used music to guide them. They had to learn this sacred song, which would lead them to their destination as they sang it."

"I like it," Vern said. "Music and stories—that's what we're about."

"Sounds like it's settled," Raig said. "Welcome to Songlines!"

Raig has deliberately kept the group small from the outset. I'd spotted the notices in the students' union about this choir performing in the hospital at the start of my third year. "Interest in health care an advantage," the notice said. I'd shown it to Therese, and ours were among more than twenty applications by the time the notices came down.

At my audition, Raig mentioned she was having a hard time finding men, so I was especially pleased to help recruit Bill, Vern, and Jonah. It helped that Vern had been dating Therese since high school, and I persuaded Jonah to join after I heard his gorgeous tenor in the shower. I recruited Bill from my psychology class. He was reluctant at first but agreed to try out once he heard that Vern and Jonah were already on board.

About Jonah and me. We've been dating since summer before last. We met at an outdoor concert in July, and nowadays I'm thinking our relationship could just be the real thing. I'm a talker, can't shut up sometimes, so I'm drawn to his quiet way of listening, his non-macho ways, his ease with himself. He's the same height as me, and he wears his hair down to his collar, also like me. A bit out of fashion maybe, but I love it. Only his is straight and dark and mine is the colour of yellow corn and naturally curly.

Hard to imagine that by this time next year this wonderful period of my life will be history. Hopefully I'll be starting my first year of med school and Jonah will be in grad school. We're planning to both apply to schools in the Maritimes and Ontario, and we may have to cast the net even wider. Even just getting an interview with a med school selection committee is tough, so I'm planning to apply to naturopathic schools too. For the past two summers I've worked at a health food store in Gananoque, and I learned all kinds of things about nutrition, botanicals, homeopathy, acupuncture, essential oils, you name it.

Jocelyn, the naturopath who owns the store, told me about her own experience. "They said after my interview at Summerhill med school that they were putting me on their alternates list. They were almost certain I'd get in the next year. But I wasn't about to wait it out, so I applied to the naturopathic school in Toronto, and they took me right off."

I especially liked the idea of healing the whole body with natural remedies, though I sometimes wonder how much of a place they're finding in medical school training. Modern medicine seems to be all about high-powered diagnostic tools, drugs, and surgery, with the patient in danger of getting forgotten altogether. Which is why Raig started Songlines in the first place. Some of my favourite times with Jonah are when we talk about the patients we've met—not about their diagnoses or medical treatments, simply about them as people whose full and busy lives have had to be put on hold. I may be a science nerd, but I'm more interested in the people themselves than I am in their diagnoses.

Two

"Okay, let's take a break," says Raig.

As I settle around the table with the others, I can feel the energy that singing together has released. Most of us pull out our notepads or journals, but Dawn gets her knitting needles from her bag, together with a couple of feet of black and gold scarf. She's told us that she started knitting back in second grade and has just kept going.

The special part of rehearsal for all of us is the sharing circle afterwards. Singing as a group loosens up everyone's emotions, regardless of the kind of week we've had—in and out of the classroom. Even Amy and Carole are often willing to open up some about their lives.

From the top of the table, Raig looks around at the group. "I know most of you plan a career in health care, but Dawn, you're set on making music your career, right?"

"Yes. Actually, I've been exploring some more about music therapy. It's health care too—just a different way of looking at it. Good for whatever's wrong with you—body, mind, and spirit. But you need to have an instrument—something easily portable—not just a good voice. Bill's been giving me guitar lessons, and I've been playing and singing on the wards a few times. Widening my range, you might say."

Dawn and Bill haven't talked about it, but I think their relationship goes a bit further than guitar lessons. I find myself hoping so, because Bill is a Scot from way back and I never pictured him dating a black woman.

"We've got to hear more about that," Raig says. "I hope you're keeping a record of your experiences?"

"Yup. In my journal. I'll be sure to report back some more."

"Jonah, what about you?" Raig directs her attention to my boyfriend at the other end of the table. "I don't think you've ever told us your career plans."

Jonah pulls his attention from the notebook he's been jotting in. He's wearing his standard uniform of T-shirt and jeans, but the tee is one I haven't seen before. Dark grey, with a large maroon image of what looks like an anatomically correct heart right in the middle.

"Thanks for asking. You're right, I haven't said too much. I have had a few ideas, but I've finally settled on taking a Master's in anthropology. Maybe even go for a Ph.D. I've really enjoyed my undergrad classes— especially cultural anthropology. I'm interested in studying the music of different cultures."

"Tell us a bit more, if you're willing."

"Sure." Jonah looks around at the group. "Well, I guess we've all heard Canada described as a mosaic. I mean, we've got a growing population of Indigenous Peoples, along with a mix of immigrants and settlers from all over the world, with different traditions, languages, beliefs, you name it. I'm putting together my senior thesis on some of the effects of this. Big subject, I know, but I'm honing down on music in particular. I'm planning to interview, I don't know, maybe twenty students from diverse backgrounds. Hopefully all studying different subjects across campus. I want to look at what music is important to them, and why. What music they grew up with and what they think about music in a social and cultural context. Then see what it all tells me—what they have in common as well as some of the contrasts."

I'm delighted Raig has asked Jonah to talk about himself, because he is so much more a listener than a talker. We've chatted a good bit about our career plans, including how likely it is we can get into graduate programs in the same city—ideally right here in Halifax. But I feel a particular thrill listening to my boyfriend address the whole group. He is so calm and clear—like he's really thought it through.

He stops talking, and I know he feels he's taken up enough airtime. He smiles shyly as he looks out at us all.

After a silence, Raig says, "Wow, I've uncovered a rich vein with you and Dawn. Thanks. We'll certainly want to hear more from both of you this semester." She looks down the table at everyone. "Okay, so it doesn't matter what you're planning to do with your lives. It's hugely important that you can say in your job applications or your grad school interview or whatever how you've spent these semesters volunteering with people who are ill. Patients of all ages with all kinds of problems. Learning the stories of their lives—not just about their diseases. And hopefully making art with them so they discover how healing it can be. That experience can carry as much weight as a high grade point average." She pauses. "And never forget—we're all going to get sick, and we're all going to look to others for help. It's our human condition."

"You know who I'll look to first," Therese says. "It's those nurses. Just watching them working with their patients has helped me see how the world goes around in hospitals."

Therese is the calming voice in my ear whenever I find myself getting too worked up. She and I got paired together in first year when we were living in residence, and we decided to stay together when we found a nice little basement apartment near the Public Gardens and a short walk to the university. Not that that mattered for our second year, when the campus was shut down and classes were all online.

"Yes, you can probably learn more from a nurse than from any doctor," Raig says, grinning. "But don't tell the docs I said so! Okay, so who else has something to share? Remember, whatever you say in this room stays in this room, right?"

Everyone nods. We all know the rules: Don't interrupt, don't judge, just listen. And above all, don't gossip about anything you hear.

"I had a lovely time again with Chi-Chi," Vern offers. "She's looking much better, getting her appetite back. She's a lovely little girl. Then I worked with this older patient who is essentially deaf. He's got a bit of hearing left, but he relies mostly on sign language, so he's teaching me. I tried painting a T-shirt with him, but he wasn't too excited about it. I told him I was a biology major, not an artist, so if I could do it, he could too. I had a hard time getting through to him, though. I kept remembering what you've told us—let the patient take the lead, however long it takes."

"Tough sometimes, though," Raig says, "especially with the older men."

"Yeah. It helps a lot when I let him take over and teach me some new signs for words. I guess because he feels like he's in charge. And it gets us laughing a whole lot!"

"Hey, that reminds me," says Dawn. "I know this woman, she used to teach in the music department, but now she's started a theatre group with people who have hearing and speaking challenges. Mostly children but a few adults too. She started it for deaf people, but she's adapted it to hearing people as well. It's great—a wonderful mix of acting and dancing and mime, along with the signing. Sally, the director, stands up front on the side of the stage. She speaks any parts you can't easily understand visually. But she doesn't have to do much of that—it's like watching a silent Charlie Chaplin movie."

"That sounds so cool," I say. "And I agree, Vern, having your patient teach you something new is really fun." I pull out my multi-coloured papier mâché mask from my backpack. "I brought this along as another project we can do with our buddies. A lot of people find mask-making a lot more fun than painting T-shirts."

"Hey, I'd like to try that," says Bill, who is sitting next to me. I hand him the mask and he turns it over in his massive hands. "What do you need in the way of materials?"

"Let's see. Well, scissors, glue, construction paper—black works best. Markers, glitter, sequins—you name it. There's an instruction sheet in the art office. Good for ages six to ninety-six!"

Bill passes it on around the group. "I like this kind of stuff. I've been looking for new ideas." He looks up at Raig. "I know you always tell us we're really just there to be someone to hang out with. But it's a whole lot easier when you've got a task to work on together. Especially with some of the older patients, like you said."

"What about you, Amy?" Raig must have noticed she hasn't been paying much attention. "Do you have anything to report?"

Amy looks up briefly. Her eyes are glittering behind her glasses, like she's ready to burst into tears—which wouldn't be the first time. We all know she struggles with bouts of depression and that being a member of Songlines has been as good as taking a pill for it.

"Not too much. I'm going to pass, okay?"

"Sure."

It's just fine not to offer too much at these sessions. Just showing up at all can be an effort—even getting out of bed each morning. At least one other choir member besides Amy is regularly seeing one of the student counsellors.

"I've got something I want to share." Everyone knows Carole has been working with Mrs. Tate, who isn't expected to be around much longer. Carole's eyes are already moist as she starts to talk, and she's having a hard time getting the words out. She and Amy are close, and I sense she's affected by her friend's mood. She opens her journal and starts to read.

"Mrs. Tate was transferred up to ICU last night. I went to see her. I had the art supplies for the project we've been working on together, but they wouldn't let me in. Only family, they told me. Well, I feel like I'm pretty much family, but they couldn't even tell me what was happening. She's my gran's age, and I still miss my gran."

Carole stops talking, her tears flowing freely. Everyone stays quiet, not rushing to comfort her or halt her crying. We all know this is what we're here for—to share our feelings like this. And most of us have already gone through the pain of losing a patient we'd been working with for a while. You couldn't be part of Songlines and not get close to them. That was the whole point.

"Okay," says Raig, once it seems like enough time has elapsed, "let's warm up our voices. After three—garlic gargle, gargle with garlic; garlic gargle, gargle with garlic….abominable abdominals, abominable abdominals, abominable abdominals…. Faster, faster," she urges us. Without a pause for breath, we are into "lemon liniment, lemon liniment, lemon liniment…." Raig keeps pouring on the tongue twisters at a faster and faster pace until we are all stumbling and guffawing and holding onto each other for support.

"Okay, I think we're ready to head down to the atrium," she announces.

As we gather up our backpacks and head out, Carole is holding onto the hugs that Amy and Therese and Dawn offer her. There's no room for me, so I go and hug Jonah instead.

Three

I take the three flights of stairs behind the others down to the hospital atrium, thinking back to when the choir had first come together.

"I'm not thinking big performances at the standard university venues, or touring around the province," Raig had told us. "My idea is to bring you students into the hospital. I know how healing it can be to make art of any kind. Especially making music—or simply listening to it. We'll meet once a week to rehearse and chat together, then we'll do a short performance in the hospital atrium. They already have a piano there, which isn't getting much of a workout. After performing you'll spend time with your patient buddies, learn their stories, be a support to them beyond their families and the hospital staff."

Raig began by taking us room-to-room on the children's wards, because as a child life worker she was a familiar face to all the staff. There were still lingering effects of the whole COVID thing, so we had to be masked, scrub our hands before entering the ward, and we weren't allowed directly into any of the patients' rooms. But we could group ourselves in the passageways outside, and a boisterous version of "Hakuna Matata" or "Baby Beluga" always brought cheers from the children and their families.

Our impromptu choir really bonded when Anthea, the head nurse, suggested we go visit Eli. The fourteen-year-old had developed leukemia, and his brother, Carl, a year younger, was there every day once school was out.

"I've already told Eli you might be coming by," Anthea told us. "He and his brother started their own rock band in their garage a while back with a couple of friends. Eli got very sick—I can't tell you too much about that, but he was in a coma for a good while. Then his brother started playing some of their songs and it seemed like it revived him."

There was a big sign on the door warning us to stay out, so five of us gathered in the doorway while Raig joined Carl at Eli's bedside. He was sleeping soundly and had an intravenous line running into the port the surgeons had sewn in below his collarbone. "Saves him getting stuck in his arms all the time," Raig explained to us. We sang a couple of songs we had been practicing, then asked Carl what he thought Eli would like to hear.

"Any Beatles numbers," he'd answered promptly. "We both know most of them and play them a lot."

We sang "Let it Be," with Carl joining in on his guitar. It was like magic: as the song drew to a close, Eli opened his eyes and grinned sleepily at each of us in turn. That woke all of us up to what a powerful effect the right kind of music can have.

A short while later, Chloe, the artist who ran the hospital's Arts Smarts program, approached Raig about us performing at one of the regular events they held at noon every Friday.

"We invite solo musicians from the community to perform, and poets and writers often do a reading. But a student choir would be a real draw," Chloe told Raig. "I should warn you, there's no set audience—might be just a handful of people. This isn't like a concert people buy tickets for. You'll usually be singing to passersby, and most of them are in a hurry to get where they're going. But the rule is, when twelve noon strikes, on with the show!"

For our first Friday performance there was only a scattering of people sitting on benches eating their lunch. Chloe was warming things up with old favourites at the piano when we arrived. We spread ourselves out on either side as Raig introduced us, making sure we stayed at least six feet from our audience.

"We'll sing a few numbers, then we'll be happy to take requests. But only well-known ones, mind—we're not professionals with a big repertoire. We really want you to join in too. Remember: harmonizing is just singing any note that no one else is singing!"

By the time our allotted half-hour was over, the crowd had more than doubled. A few nurses stopped by to listen, as well as staff from the out-patient pharmacy just beyond the atrium. There had been several requests, most of which we could handle, and there were more than a few teary faces among the laughter and applause. The singing and shared stories had taken everyone a few steps further along on their healing journey.

Four

"I'm heading up to the teen lounge to see Darlene," I tell Therese and Jonah as we stand in line at the hospital cafeteria after our first Friday noon performance of the new term. "She's in overnight for her regular transfusion. You got time to join me?"

"Sure. Actually, I told Jackie I'd look for her there about now," Therese says as she sticks a plastic spoon into her dish of frozen yogurt. "I promised her a new pedicure."

The teen lounge is the regular meeting place for the peer program Raig has signed us up for. Our buddies are mostly adolescents with illnesses they will likely never recover from—diabetes, cystic fibrosis, sickle cell disease, cancer, and some rarer ones. We have to commit to spending time one-on-one with our patient buddies at least once a week as long as they're in hospital. Some of us make home visits, too, if our patients live close enough.

Mostly when we meet up, we simply hang out, play video games, watch movies, and talk with our buddies about how things are going with their diabetes or sickle cell or whatever. But we also chat about their lives beyond the hospital walls, knowing the last thing most of them want to talk about is what put them in here. They already spend altogether too much time thinking about their illness—when they aren't talking to their doctors and nurses about it.

Raig encourages us to share something of our own lives too, especially if we find it hard to keep the conversation going. Every adolescent is interested in the goings-on of university students—probably imagining one continuous round of drunken partying. But these get-togethers soon become a source of emotional support. Access to professional counselling is way too limited for these teens—even if they are open to the idea. The psych and social work people always seem to have more than they can handle, so they're delighted to have us students as backup. Raig has newcomers to the choir meet with one of the psychology faculty to get pointers about how to work with the patients. Many of the patients are only a handful of years younger than us and are already in the throes of adolescent angst, without having an incurable disease thrown on top.

I follow Jonah and Therese as we make our way to the takeout counter, aware of the line forming behind us as we put in our lunch orders. "How's Jackie doing?" I ask Therese.

"She's scared. She'll be graduating to the adult CF program next month, and she thinks she won't get the same kind of care and attention she's been used to in pediatrics. She's probably right, but I've promised I won't desert her. It's good she lives only just out of town, so I can make the odd house call in between her trips to hospital."

"What age do they move on to the adult program?"

"Nineteen, I think," Therese answers. "Or else when they graduate from high school. Darlene's got thalassemia, hasn't she?" she asks, referring to my own patient buddy.

"Right. I guess it's the same for teens like her—I mean about moving up from peds to the adult program. Anyway, she's still got a couple of years to go. Her home's maybe a forty-five-minute drive, but I made the trip to see her one time, got to meet her family. It's real handy having a boyfriend with a truck to get us around." I bump shoulders with Jonah and grin at him. He wraps an arm about my waist.

"I enjoyed the trip," he says. "I don't think my patient will be making it home any time soon. I haven't figured out what's wrong with him exactly, but I know that's not what I'm there for."

"Darlene has a younger sister and brother," I tell them, "but neither of them has thalassemia. They call her Darl, so I'm learning to do so too. Darl's brother is only about thirteen, but he's already taller than she is."

"Is it because of her illness that she hasn't grown much?" Therese asks.

"Yes. It seems the extra iron in the blood from the transfusions she's had over the years gets deposited all over her body—bones, liver, heart— and her hormone glands too. She doesn't make enough growth hormone or other hormones to mature properly."

"Does that mean she might not live as long as most of us?"

"That's right." Raig doesn't encourage us to read up about our patients' illnesses, but I wanted to know more about Darl's situation. "From what I've read, most people with the worst form of thalassemia, like Darl, die as young adults."

"That really sucks," says Jonah.

"Yeah. I try not to think about it too much—and she's never brought it up to me," I tell them. "Maybe she'll want to open up more later. I just hope I can handle it. Darl told me they've been looking for a donor for a stem cell transplant. A good few people with thalassemia have been cured that way. There's a big medical centre in Italy that's done a lot of transplants. It's because the disease shows up mostly in Mediterranean families, or people who come from there—Italy and Greece especially. Man, genes are weird. I've only had one genetics class, but there's a whole lot to learn."

I stop talking, realizing people around us could be listening in. A real no-no, Raig has told us—talking about patients and their diseases in earshot of strangers. I wait till the three of us have grabbed a table in the corner out of earshot and laid out our spoils. Jonah picks up the subject.

"Ellen was telling me about stem cell transplants," he says to Therese. "How they would give Darlene a mega dose of chemotherapy to pretty much wipe out her bone marrow, then give her an infusion of new marrow cells from a healthy donor—and her thalassemia would be gone forever. Amazing, eh? But it seems like it's much harder to find good matches for patients with mixed heritage like Darlene. Go figure."

"It's great visiting at home though, right?" Therese says. "I told my granddad about it—he was in family practice all his life. He said even in his day it was getting harder and harder to make home visits, especially in a rural practice with patients scattered over a wide area. He envies me." She grins at us both. "Jackie's got two younger sisters, and all three of them help their mom with the cooking and cleaning and stuff. The couple of times I've made it out there they've made supper for me. Jackie's mom says she knows we students eat nothing but junk food!"

"Not far wrong." I eye the burger and fries I'm sharing with Jonah. "One great thing, though. I know Darlene won't mind me telling you—she's real proud of it. She just had her first period. A number of the teens with thalassemia never even go through puberty. It's to do with the excess iron that collects in their ovaries from all the donated blood."

We bus our table and head out of the cafeteria. As we get to the line of elevators, Jonah reaches to press the button. I stop him.

"Come on, babe—stairs, remember?"

"Yeah, you're right." He grins. "Three flights are no big deal for you. But my buddy is up in Geriatrics on the sixth floor!"

"Well, take a break with us on the third." I eye his slim frame. "Not that you're in much danger of getting fat!"

We pause on the landing on the third floor, and I kiss Jonah goodbye before he heads on upstairs. The teen room is crowded when Therese and I enter, making sure our masks are in place, and we give our hands a thorough wash. The pool table is busy as always, and the bean bag chairs are occupied with teens playing video games. There are a couple of unoccupied computers in what's called "cyberspace" by the windows.

"Amazing how good these guys get at juggling their IV poles," I say to Therese as we greet several familiar faces.

"Here I am, Therese," Jackie yells from a bean bag across the room. "I'm all set—and a couple of others want you to do their nails too. They were blown away with what you did with mine last time."

"Sure thing! But it doesn't look like there's too much space around here," Therese calls back to her. "Let's head back to your room."

"Hey, what about me?" It was one of the guys. I think his name is Al, and I know from his bald head he has cancer. "My toes could do with a touch-up—maybe scarlet with green spots. What d'you think?"

"Sure, no problem." Therese grins at him as she helps Jackie manoeuvre her IV pole through the door on the way to her room. "Can't hurt, might catch on!"

I look around for Darlene but see no sign of her. She's probably hooked up to her transfusion back in her room. I follow Jackie and Therese out the door and down the corridor. Darlene's bed is in the four-bed bay next to Jackie's room. Darlene greets me with a grin and a one-armed hug. Her other arm is splinted and wrapped, partly concealing the IV line disappearing into a vein on her forearm. A full plastic bag of blood is suspended from a pole close to her bed.

I watch the steady crimson drip for a long moment. It never ceases to fascinate me how the scientists of a century ago uncovered the secrets of human blood types. How easy and safe it is today to pick out the right donor every time Darlene needs this life-giving infusion. Down to every three weeks now, I just heard—what a life sentence. Finding the right bone marrow donor is a whole other problem.

"Here, Darlene, I've brought you some fries straight from the cafeteria. I don't need them all."

I spread paper towels and a couple of paper plates on the blanket and lay out equal portions for each of us.

"What's new with you?" I ask.

"Not too much. I get to skip school for the day."

"I guess that's one good thing about coming in here every few weeks."

We chat for a few more minutes, then Raig appears at the door. She beckons me over and speaks quietly.

"D'you think you can take on another patient? I think you're the best one to be this guy's buddy. He might be quite a challenge. Dylan's his name—a seventeen-year-old with sickle cell disease. He's pretty pissed off with life. Been in for five days, but I've only just got him to wake up and chat a bit."

"Sure. I've got a class in an hour, so I'll go by and see him right after my visit with Darl."

"Great. And don't be put off if it takes a lot to rouse him. He's in with a bad pain crisis so he's wrapped 24-7 in the comforting arms of morphine."

A few minutes later I head past the nurses' station, greeting a couple of familiar faces on my way to Dylan's room. I find my new buddy-to-be sacked out, facing the window. He has pulled his bed covers up almost over his head. I think back to all the tips I've been taught about how to approach a new patient.

Soon after Raig set up the buddy program, she arranged for us to meet with a prof called Bart from the university's theatre department. She had hit on the idea of our learning from an actor about making connections with a person we'd never met. Bart works with Arts Smarts, the hospital's artists-in-residence program, and teaches a lot of artists the kinds of skills actors need. How to connect with other people, how fast to move, introducing yourself by name and shaking hands—and a whole lot more.

"We're going to use role play," Bart told us at our training session. "Just like we actors do onstage all the time. Doctors and nurses have to play parts too, but that doesn't make the situation any less real."

We'd been reluctant at first, embarrassed to perform in front of our colleagues. "Better get over that pretty quick," Bart chided us, "if you're going to be any good in real life situations."

He asked us to pair up and had one of us play the patient and the other the doctor. "Now, imagine you've just found out something bad is going down with your patient," he told the doctor-actor. "Let's say their new X-ray results aren't good. You're going to open the door, walk across the room, greet the patient, find a place to sit down, and break the news to them." He turned to the other student. "Now, I need you as the patient to react so it'll seem like the real thing. Don't worry, guys, there's no one else here, just the three of us." Which had made our whole group guffaw, mostly with discomfort.

Bart had had us try out different options. "Just how do you open the door? Briskly, like you're in charge? Or tentatively, so as not to scare your patient? What kind of signals do you give? How fast do you move toward the bedside? Do you shake hands? How do you introduce yourself?" We don't know when we might be faced with COVID rules again. He looked around at the whole group to make sure this was sinking in.

"You sit down, right—never stand and loom over your patient. But how close? What feels like the right distance? Then do you get straight to the point, or do you chat about things in general before coming to the big reason you're here? Do you touch your patient? And what about how fast you speak—do you pause between each sentence? Then you have to think about how you leave the room at the end. Lots of things to consider, right? Actors rehearse all this stuff every time they go on stage."

We glanced at each other. This was totally new territory. We all agreed it was a bit easier being in the role of the patient. We even found ways to help our classmates adapt their performance so they became more genuine and compassionate. Each of us got totally flustered trying to keep all of Bart's directions in mind when we were in the doctor role. It felt to me like when I had first taken driving lessons, having never been behind the wheel of a car before.

"This stuff doesn't come naturally," Bart reminded us. "It takes a lot of practice to get good at it. Why d'you think we actors do so much rehearsing?"

I wondered whether we'd get taught any of this in med school.

Five

I find Paula, Dylan's nurse, before I head in to see Dylan. She confirms he's getting an around-the-clock infusion of morphine.

"It's pretty much standard with the sickle cell patients when they come in with a pain crisis," the nurse tells me. "You might have a hard time getting much out of him. Oh, and it's change of shift right now, so Dylan will have a new nurse arriving any time."

I pull a chair up close to my would-be buddy's bedside so I'm facing him. His covers are pulled right up and the morphine infusion is dripping steadily into his left arm. He doesn't stir from his slumber. I go over in my mind all I have learned from Bart about approaching a new patient. I nudge him gently. "Hi, Dylan. I just came to visit. I know you're pretty sleepy, but I was hoping we could chat a bit."

No response. I lay my hand on the top of his blanket and try again.

"I hear you've been sleeping pretty solidly the past couple of days. Maybe you can tell me about what's been happening with you."

He stirs briefly without opening his eyes. "Who wants to know?"

I feel some small encouragement that I've at least elicited a response. I press on.

"My name's Ellen. I'm a student here at the university. I thought maybe you'd like to have someone to hang out with. I hear you don't get many visitors."

"Shit, not one of those medical students! How come you can't just let me sleep?"

"No, no. I'm not a medical student. Maybe one day but not yet. I'm not here to examine you or anything like that. I just thought you might like a little company."

Silence. Dylan's eyes remain closed.

"I've heard a bit about what's been happening to you. About your pain crisis and stuff. I'd really like to hear what it's like. It can help to talk about things that are hard to deal with."

He finally flicks his eyes open. "Goes with the f-ing territory, right?" he mutters. "I got stuck with this f-ing disease, so I end up spending half my life in this f-ing dungeon. Just my crap luck. And all they do is stick me on these painkillers, which half the time don't do diddly-shit." His words are coming out slurred. I pull my chair up even closer.

"I'm sorry you're having such a hard time, Dylan. Maybe they'll come up with something new to try. Something that will work better."

"Whole lot of good that'll do. You don't get shot of sickle cell. I'm stuck with it." He's starting to pull himself up in the bed using his free right arm. I reach to help but quickly decide he might resent any such move on my part.

"They put me back up in Intensive Care last time. My lungs were clogging up. Came close to croaking from pneumonia. Might have been better if I had."

I lean back in my chair. I seem to have got him going. A bleak response is better than none at all. I remember Raig saying that when patients get mad, it's almost never you they are mad at. Rather it's their whole situation.

"Then there was this bunch of students, or new doctors—who knows?—down in Emerg last time I was in. Didn't know shit about me and of course didn't have my chart handy. They saw all the scars on my arms, from where other docs had tried getting IVs started. Of course I have to be some kind of drug addict, don't I? Or worse, a pusher. Didn't help that I know all my drugs pretty well, even the doses. I tell them what I need, and how maybe they could give me a few doses of OxyContin to go home with. That really got 'em going."

Dylan seems to be building up a head of steam. His voice is getting louder and hoarser. He reaches for the box of tissues on his bed table and starts hawking up tacky spit. He grabs at his ribs, wincing at the pain the coughing has brought on. I cast about in my mind for ways I might help him deal with all this resentment at the world. At even being born, it seems like.

A young nurse appears at the door, then moves to the other side of Dylan's bed. I remember Paula telling me he would have a new nurse for the evening shift. She's very pretty, with glowing skin the colour of dark roasted coffee.

"Hi, Dylan," she says. "My name's Beatrix, I'm your new nurse. I just came to say hey, see how you're doing." She looks over at me. "But I don't want to interrupt your conversation. I can come back later."

"No, no, it's just fine," I tell her quickly. I'd noticed that Dylan has fastened his full attention on Beatrix. The nurse smiles at me, then speaks again to her patient. "How is your pain level, Dylan—out of ten?"

The hacking into tissues ceases abruptly. He grasps a cup of water from his bed table and swallows several large gulps. Giving himself time to think how to respond, I suspect.

"I guess maybe it's eased some. Down to a five." I want to smile. He hadn't been about to admit that to me. Male pride kicking in?

"Well, that's really good to hear, Dylan."

Beatrix promptly perches herself on the edge of his bed. "I haven't been around too many guys with sickle cell, so maybe you can teach me a bit about it."

"Yeah, sure. I know about everything there is to know. It's a killer, I'll tell you that."

Dylan's surliness has vanished. But I'm pretty sure it isn't just that he's suddenly feeling less pain, or how nice his new nurse is toward him; her stunning looks surely have a lot to do with it. I ease myself back in my chair and let the scene play out.

"Do many people come to see you when you're in hospital?" Beatrix asks.

"What's it look like? My mom, she's probably out with her latest. And my dad, he's been gone forever—we're not in touch. I can't hardly keep up with my buds, what with being in and out of this place."

"No girlfriends?"

"I never had a date." Dylan's voice has dropped to a whisper. "No girl's ever going to want me."

"Don't you be so sure," Beatrix says. "Lots of girls want to hang out with guys who've had more than their share of tough breaks."

"Life sucks, you know?"

Dylan looks on the brink of tears. Beatrix doesn't hesitate. She reaches her hand out and lays it on his arm.

"I'm real sorry this happened to you. I hear you're in quite a bit. I expect I'll be looking after you again."

"That'd be good."

"Look, I've got something I want to share with you, Dylan. Something I don't usually talk about with my patients. You see, in my last year in high school I got this really bad problem in my gut—my bowel. And they diagnosed it as ulcerative colitis—which is a bad scene. Turns out it quite often affects teens or young adults. Not that a whole lot of people get it—I just happened to draw the short straw.

"I had to have this surgery, just around my eighteenth birthday. I ended up with a bit of my bowel sewed to the outside of my belly—so I could still go to the bathroom. Because they'd had to cut out the far end of my intestine. A stoma, they call that piece that sticks out of me. Some birthday gift, eh?"

Beatrix stops talking, stands up from the bed and starts to ease down the rim of her pants. On the right side of her abdomen, close to where her belly button would normally have been, there's a long pink scar disappearing under a pouch lying snug against her side.

"This is where the poop comes out. I get to empty it several times a day. And I'm stuck with it—like forever."

She promptly tugs her pants back up and drops her smock back in place. She grins at Dylan and me in turn. "But what I want to tell you, Dylan—it hasn't screwed up my social life one bit."

Dylan is totally silenced. He gazes at Beatrix with open admiration. I myself feel an impulse to burst out clapping. Wow, that was some teaching session. And talk about a way to get your patient's attention. Not that anyone would ever wish such a thing to happen to a teenage girl. But I'll never forget the look of regard on Dylan's face as Beatrix leaves. I can't begin to imagine any doctor ever showing off his stoma to a patient. Well, if this is nursing care, maybe it's time to rethink my options—if I don't get into med school, that is.

Six

October

It's raining hard at seven thirty on Friday night as Vern drops me and Therese outside the entrance to the Shellfish Grill on the corner of South Park Street and University Avenue.

"See if you can grab a table while Bill and I hunt up a parking spot," Vern says as we scramble out the back. "Or maybe Dawn or someone is already here." Vern glances at Bill in the passenger seat. "You got your umbrella handy?"

"Yeah, no worries." Bill grins. "What's a little downpour to start off our evening?"

I'm delighted that Jonah's twenty-second birthday falls on a Friday this year—with the whole weekend stretching ahead of us. This will be our third birthday celebration together, following Jonah's twenty-first last year, and my twenty-first in February. And who knows where we'll both be this time next year. Jonah has his cultural anthropology class late on Fridays, and he isn't about to skip it even for his birthday bash. I'm very intrigued with his senior thesis about the place of music in different cultures. Ethnomusicology is the word he is fond of dropping into our conversation. "The only seven-syllable word I know," he likes to tell people.

The Grill is already getting crowded, but Therese spots a table and three free seats right behind the door. The table hasn't been cleared yet, the last occupants must have just left.

"Looks like our luck's in," I yell over the noise. "Twenty thousand students in this university, and we've scored a vacant table! You take up possession, Therese, and I'll try and grab a couple more chairs."

Vern and Bill join us ten minutes later, draping their wet jackets over the backs of the two additional seats I've managed to grab. We're expecting at least six people altogether. A waitress arrives to bus our table and take our drinks order. I think I recognize her from one of my classes last year, but she's really hustling and I decide this isn't a good time to start a conversation. We're halfway through our drinks when she's back for our food orders. I glance at my watch. We've been here twenty minutes already, and Jonah's class should be well over by now—though it isn't unusual for that particular professor to run late. I know Jonah will head back to his apartment to freshen up. I try his cell, first texting then calling, but get only his voice mail.

"He'll be here soon, don't worry," Therese tells me. "Maybe he forgot his wallet or his phone or something and had to go back to the apartment."

"Yeah, I guess. But it's not like him not to answer his cell when he sees it's me."

Our food comes and another half hour goes by, by which time I'm seriously worried. "I'll head over to our place," Vern suggests, "see if he's left his cell there. You guys stay here in case he shows."

Vern returns fifteen minutes later. "There's no sign he's recently been home. And neither his wallet nor his phone was there."

Therese gasps, staring at her own phone. "Ellen, is that Jonah's truck?" The image on her phone is from a news flash. There are two Mounties and several spectators watching as a tow truck hooks up a vehicle that's clearly been involved in an accident.

I grab the phone from her. "Oh, shit! It sure looks like it, but I can't see any sign of Jonah."

"I guess we'd better check Emerg," Therese says quietly. "Can you give us a ride there, Vern? Bill, do you mind staying here? Hopefully that's not Jonah's truck and he'll come through those doors any minute."

The staff nurse in the Emergency Room is sympathetic when we explain who we are.

"I can't give you any medical information, you understand," she tells us. "But yes, your friend was admitted here a while ago. He's just been moved up to the ward."

"Which ward? I'm his fiancée, surely you can tell me what's happened?"

I'm stretching the truth. Neither Jonah nor I has openly broached the subject of a permanent relationship, but I've found myself thinking more than once about this possibility. This seems like a good time to pull out the fiancée card.

"Well, I can tell you that he's in the ICU—seventh floor. It looks like he had some kind of seizure, but he was definitely starting to come around when they left here."

We meet with similar resistance in Intensive Care. Yes, your friend is here, but we can't give any medical details. And only relatives can visit. On further pressing, the receptionist at the desk tells us they have located the family. I'm starting to shake, my mind is doing jumping jacks. The three of us slump in plastic seats in the waiting area till Jonah's parents show up. Therese puts her arm around me. A shimmer of water masks my vision. I try to blink it away.

"I've never gone to Jonah's house, but it's in Port Hawkesbury, I think," Vern offers. "Isn't that right, Ellen?"

"Why didn't I think of that right off?" I straighten myself from Therese's shoulder. "I think I put his home phone number in my contact list. I've never been to Jonah's house, but he gave me their number when he was home for a while last summer."

I get Sophie, Jonah's fifteen-year-old sister, on the phone. I've heard all about her, though we've never met. I introduce myself and explain that we're at the university hospital. Sophie sounds very scared. She confirms that her mom is on the way to the hospital.

"She left maybe an hour and half ago," she says. "Have you got any news about how he's doing?"

I explain the situation and tell her I'm sure her mom will be in touch as soon as she hears anything. More than an hour passes before Jonah's mom comes out of the elevator and immediately recognizes me. We had met last semester when she came to visit. She hugs me and Vern and Therese introduce themselves. Vern offers her his seat.

"No, no, I'm going straight in. I'll come right out as soon as I have any news to share."

Vern calls Bill to update him, then heads off to get us coffee from the hospital cafeteria. I make several circuits of the waiting area between bouts of sobbing on Therese's shoulder. It seems like several hours go by, but in reality it's less than thirty minutes before Jonah's mother reappears through the ICU door.

"You can come on in, Ellen, but just for a short while," she tells me as she removes her face mask. "I had to twist the nurse's arm a bit to get the okay. Look, they don't know too much yet, but he's come around and he knew me at once. They're pretty sure he had an epileptic seizure." She keeps talking as we head into the ICU. "He's never ever had one before, but the resident doctor said that could happen. He had some kind of brain scan done almost as soon as he got here, but they need to repeat it. He was too restless for them to get good pictures."

One of the nurses at once hands me a face mask and points me to the washroom to give my hands a thorough scrubbing. I realize this isn't some left-over COVID rule, just normal procedure till they know more about what's happening with Jonah. His room is right opposite the nurses' station. As I enter, I take in the intravenous line running into his left arm and the side rails raised on each side of the bed. His eyes are closed, but he opens them as soon as I pull down my face mask and kiss his right eyelid, then his cheek. He summons a lopsided grin.

"Some birthday bash, eh?"

I feel a surge of relief hearing his voice. It seems slurred but maybe that's because he's still coming around from whatever happened.

"Oh, Jonah, I was so scared. How are you, babe?"

"Okay, I guess. Just this splitting headache. Don't remember a thing about how I got here. The nurse said I had a seizure, and the cops thought I was drunk. My birthday, and we didn't get to party, but I get an unexpected visit from my mom instead!"

His mother is standing right behind me. "Didn't want to miss your big day, kid!"

I grasp Jonah's free hand, manage to hold back my tears. I feel his mom's arm wrap around my shoulders.

"How's my truck?" Jonah asks.

"We'll find it," his mother says, "see what the damage is. Don't you go worrying about it."

"Guess I'm lucky I didn't get hurt more. I'm trying to figure out what happened. It's still a blank. I don't even remember getting into the truck to join you, Ellen."

"The police gave me the keys," Jonah's mother tells him. "And I've got your wallet and cellphone."

The nurse we had talked to outside appears. She moves to the other side of the bed.

"I'm Suze, Jonah—you remember me from earlier, right?" she says. "How's it going with you?"

"Good, I guess. I'm just confused. And my head's hurting pretty bad."

"That can happen after a seizure. I'm sorry, we can't give you any more pain meds right now. Not till we know a bit more about what happened."

Suze looks over at me and Jonah's mom. "I told Jonah what the police told us, but I don't think he was taking it in. It seems like he lost control of his truck on University Avenue. Can't have been going too fast, given all the traffic out there. When the police arrived, they thought he was sleeping off a bout of heavy drinking. There didn't seem to be any danger of a fire starting, so they had his vehicle towed to the Shell garage close by. You should be able to find it pretty easily."

She looks back at Jonah. "Apparently they had you in handcuffs when they brought you into Emerg! But they figured out pretty quick your accident had nothing to do with alcohol or drugs. They did a CAT scan right off, though you were coming around by then and they couldn't get you to lie still. They'll be bringing you down for another one any time."

"You still don't know what caused…whatever happened?" Jonah's mom asks her.

"Well, the docs are pretty certain Jonah had a seizure of some sort. But you said there's no history of epilepsy in your family, so we just need to see what the scan shows." The nurse glances at me, then back at Jonah. "But try not to worry too much. You're in no immediate danger. And you seem to be recovering fast!"

"There's something else, though," Jonah says. "My left arm and leg, they're real weak."

"That can happen after a seizure too. It will likely get better after a while. You're a young guy, no reason why you couldn't be skipping about in no time."

"Twenty-two today. Some birthday present!"

"Jeez, I'm sorry. I guess you'll be having a belated celebration." She looks back at his mother and me. "But time's up for you folks. They'll be wanting your boy down in X-ray again any time now. You can check back in again later on. And I'll call you right away if there's any more news."

As we make our way back to the elevator, Jonah's mom says, "Look, call me Ann, okay? I'm very sorry we're meeting again like this. I know you must be feeling just as scared as I am. But Joe looks like he's getting back to normal from whatever happened. I'm going to check into the Holiday Inn across from the university. Let me have your cell phone number, and I'll be sure to call or text you right away if I hear anything more." She pauses. "I know you guys are very close. We're getting to think of you as part of the family."

"Thanks."

We exchange hugs as we say goodnight. I don't tell Ann that I had claimed an almost family relationship with Jonah in Emerg earlier this evening.

Seven

Therese and I stay up late into the night, neither of us able to settle to sleep.

"It's something like this makes you realize how small most of our problems are," I say to her at some point in the early hours. "All I know is, having a friend like you right here when you need them—it means so much to me."

Therese holds onto me till I finally lay back on my bed and close my eyes. The next thing I'm aware of is the ring tone on my phone.

"Jonah's wide awake, and they say he's doing fine." It's Ann's voice. "I'm on my way over there right now, but they won't let me stay more than half an hour. I'd love to have you join me, Ellen. I can wait outside the ICU till you get here."

We grab bagels and coffee on our way to the hospital. I had told Therese that she didn't need to come this time.

"Listen, I'm going to be sticking real close to you till this all gets settled, okay?" was her answer.

"Everyone should have such a friend. Thank you."

We meet up with Ann outside the ICU. "Jonah's just got back from more X-rays," she tells us. "He had to have an MRI scan this time. They needed to get a clearer look at what there was to see—anything that shouldn't be there, I guess."

We leave Therese once more occupying one of the hard plastic chairs and opening up her laptop in the waiting area. Jonah is sitting up, an IV still running into his left arm. He reaches up to hug us both, and I see at once he is barely moving that arm. As he breaks away, there's a scared look in his eyes that hadn't been there last night. I can't remember Jonah ever frightened of anything.

"Did you see the docs?" he asks us. "They were in here a few minutes back."

"Damn, I guess we just missed them," his mother answers. "What did they tell you about the scans?"

"The head guy—didn't catch his name—he said there's something in my brain." He places his free hand on the top of his head. "Somewhere around here. He said he'd need to operate to find out what it was." Jonah is having a hard time getting his words out. He looks on the verge of tearing up. "I pretty much stopped listening after that. But he's talking about trying to set it up for Monday morning."

"I'm going to go find him right away." Ann's voice holds strong, but she too is looking shaky. "I know you're an adult, Joe, but you're not taking things in too clearly right now. I need to get the full scoop. Ellen, you stay and visit with Jonah while I go find the guy in charge."

I pull my chair up close to my boyfriend's bedside, take his good hand in mine, lay my head against his shoulder.

"Oh, Jonah, I love you," I murmur, knowing my words are coming out in a muffle that he probably can't catch. I also know I've never come right out and said those very words. Is this what it takes to really fall in love with a guy—to hear him tell you he is heading for brain surgery?

Jonah leans his head up against mine. Neither of us speaks anymore. I shift my head to the corner of his top pillow and we both close our eyes. I haven't prayed much in recent times, but I find myself murmuring silently to whatever unseen power is out there. *Oh God, let it not be as bad as it sounds.*

My mind drifts back to when we first met. A bunch of frat boys had been hitting on me at the outdoor concert, all of them drunk or stoned. Jonah was suddenly there at my side, telling them to back off and stop hassling me. It looked like things might get messy, but there were plenty of security guys around, and the frat boys quickly took off looking for other targets. We introduced ourselves to each other, almost having to shout over the music.

It was The Trews, back home on a concert tour of the Maritimes, and nowadays we like to listen to them and remember that first meeting. Jonah always comments how amazing it is that music can bring memories back as if we'd just experienced them yesterday. I can instantly recall my heart skipping the first time I watched his powerful stride as he moved toward me. He told me later the reason he showed up at the exact moment was that he'd noticed me earlier and couldn't keep his eyes off me.

"I love to remember that moment—when I caught sight of you for the first time," he often says. "I even recall which song Colin MacDonald was singing right then."

Our eyes are still closed when Ann reappears a good half-hour later. Mercifully, no staff have come in the meantime to shoo me out of Jonah's room. Maybe they've changed the rules, or the nurses have forgotten about me—though that seems unlikely. Ann nudges me gently, no doubt thinking we're both asleep.

"I caught up with the doctors as they were finishing their rounds." She reaches to grasp my hand, speaking quietly not to disturb her son who is still sleeping. "The head surgeon, Dr. El Khouri, talked to me about the X-rays and what they're planning to do. The MRI scan showed there's a tumour sitting on the right side of Joe's frontal brain. It's a small one, but that's why his left arm and leg are so weak. And why he had the seizure. He couldn't tell what kind of tumour it was—if it was cancerous or not.

But he's definitely planning to operate first thing on Monday to find out exactly what it is. And remove it completely if he possibly can." Ann stops talking for a long moment to let this sink in. "I've called home to let them know what's going on."

She says no more, just sits silent beside me. I shut my eyes tight. My mind is numb. Each time I try to voice a thought, my throat clamps down on it. At last, I speak the question sitting like a block of ice in my head.

"Does he think he… can get it out?"

"He says he won't know till he's inside, where he can get a complete look at whatever it is. He thinks it will be a pretty long operation, but he has big hopes he can get it all. He doesn't seem willing to say much more."

A new nurse appears. She's holding a tray with syringes and a bunch of other equipment on it.

"I have to ask you to take off now. I'm sorry, I know you've only been here a short while." She smiles gently at us both. "This must be really hard. But we'll look after Jonah, please try to not worry too much. Your son is in the very best place."

The nurse's tenderness starts my tears flowing free. I grasp Ann's hand tighter as we leave the unit. The door to the room next to Jonah's is open and I glance in. There is a young girl in the bed, maybe six years old. That's about how old I feel right now. Like a little kid, with no control over anything. God, I'm scared.

Eight

I get to spend short spells with Jonah over the weekend before checking in with Ann early Monday morning. She tells me Jonah is already down in surgery and that she'll call as soon as she hears anything. I spend much of the day with Therese and Vern, who only have evening classes so are free until then. Therese has left a note in the offices of both our deans with a brief explanation. None of us have the energy to catch up with our patient buddies or to hit the books in the library. Mid-term exams are still three weeks off.

"Let's take a run to the provincial park," Vern suggests over scrambled eggs and toasted bagels Therese has prepared for breakfast. "The weather looks good and a walk on the beach will blow the cobwebs away. Jonah's mom will be sure to phone, Ellen, as soon as he's back from surgery."

Vern is right, it does help to be out in the fresh air and away from town. It's nearly four in the afternoon before Ann finally calls.

"They just phoned to say he's out of surgery. He was in the operating room for over six hours. The nurse said the surgeon would be up to talk to me soon."

Ann and I sit together in the ICU waiting area for a long forty minutes. We talk very little. The neurosurgeon finally comes through the ICU doors.

"I'm sorry I've kept you waiting," he tells Ann. "I wanted to hear confirmation from pathology about everything I had sent them from the operating room." He pauses to glance at me.

"Ellen is Jonah's girlfriend," Ann says. "She's almost part of our family, so I want her to sit in." Then to me: "This is Dr. El Khouri, Jonah's surgeon."

The surgeon nods at me. "Let's head to my office. We'll find seats for you both." He has a slight accent that sounds Middle Eastern. The staff have all left for the day, but one of the resident doctors brings in extra chairs from the outer office. Ann and I sit close together. Dr. El Khouri wastes no time.

"I'm very sorry to say the news is not good. Jonah has a tumour in his brain that I couldn't totally remove. Not without doing a lot more harm than good. The pathologist has just confirmed it is malignant." He pauses to fix his eyes on us. "A cancer, that is. It's called a glioma. I'm very sorry."

He says no more, as though waiting for one of us to speak. I clamp my eyes shut. A dark fog whirls inside me, banishing coherent thought. I register Ann's voice posing the question that is just starting to form itself in the cloud that is my brain.

"What's going to happen? What can you do?"

"There are several things we're going to do right away," the surgeon answers. "I shall be consulting with my colleagues in radiation therapy and in oncology first thing in the morning. We have had a lot of success with these cancers using a combination of radiation and chemotherapy—cancer drugs. And it's very possible I can operate again later on, to remove anything that is still there."

I'm still struggling to absorb his words. I'm unable to come up with a clear thought, let alone a question to pose that makes any kind of sense. My eyes are dry. Why aren't I crying?

"Can we go in to see him?" Ann says at last.

"It would be best if you didn't right now," the surgeon answers. "He won't wake up until much later, and I don't want him disturbed in any way. He's receiving strong pain medication, as well as a steroid drug—Decadron. It will help prevent his brain swelling anymore."

Over the next couple of days Ann and I are restricted to short visits. Jonah wakes up for a few minutes when we arrive. We keep the conversation away from the devastating news I'm still trying to get my head around. Jonah asks me about the choir and our patient buddies.

"Could you check in with the gentleman on Gerontology, babe, and the young guy on the adolescent floor?"

How can he find it in himself to think about his patient buddies right now? My tears jerk free. I swallow hard, struggle to compose myself.

"Of course. I'll let you know how they're doing. And the dean knows you'll be missing classes for a good bit."

Ann updates him about their family. She had broken the news on the phone to Belinda and Sophie right after our meeting with Dr. El Khouri. She told me Belinda had been frantic, but Ann had finally dissuaded her from rushing right up here, explaining that there was nothing she could do right now. Best she head off to work and try to get her mind off things. I know very little about Belinda except that she's Ann's partner. The two of them must have decided it's best Ann stay up here and handle things as they unfold while Belinda looks out for Sophie.

I decide to take a leave of absence from classes for the next couple of weeks. I'm starting to get my head around the neurosurgeon's news. I can't face my classmates or my teachers right now, or even concentrate on studying in the library. Jonah will soon be receiving the same kind of treatment as many of our patient buddies: chemotherapy and radiation.

I go and see the dean of sciences, who teaches a cell biology class I'm enrolled in.

"One of Jonah's doctors called me, so I know a bit about what's happened," he tells me. He comes around from behind his desk to sit next to me. He has two desks, one "active" and one piled high with paperwork apparently abandoned. "Look, I know you and Jonah are close, and I'm awfully sorry this has happened. You might want to go see someone at the health and wellness centre? Someone to talk to, I mean."

"Thank you, sir. Yes, that might be good."

I make my escape before I lose it. I know he means to be helpful, but I don't think he would deal well with having a bawling undergraduate in his office first thing in the morning. I quickly decide not to take him up on his suggestion. The best therapy for me right now will be to catch up with my patient buddies, as well as Jonah's two patients. Maybe it will be a distraction from the thoughts crowding in on me day and night. I especially like the pediatric ward, where there are always hordes of kids, many of them treating the place as a home-away-from-home.

I seek out Raig in the child life office. She's taking a break to catch up with her patient charts. She wraps me in her arms and I'm at once sobbing my heart out on her shoulder.

"I just heard the news on rounds this morning, Ellen," she murmurs. "You must be devastated."

I cling on as she rocks me gently back and forth in the middle of this overcrowded space. I'm dimly aware of the colourful array of books and zines, DVDs, balloons, soft toys and musical instruments all around me.

"Are they letting you visit?" Raig asks as I finally straighten up and grab a handful of tissues from the box she offers me. I dab my eyes and blow my nose several times.

"Yeah. They're treating me like family. Jonah's mom especially. She and I are visiting Jonah every morning. But they don't let us stay long." I summon a grin. "Anyway, I'm taking a break from school, and I need something to distract me. Some*one*, I mean. I'd really like to spend a bit of time with the patients."

"Got you. Maybe you'd like to meet Jonah's buddy on this floor. You're still set on getting into med school, right?" I nod. "This little fellow will be a great teacher. He loves talking about what's wrong and what the docs are doing for him."

"That would be good. Jonah already asked me to fill in as his buddy."

Nine

As we enter the ward, we almost trip over a young boy in a wheelchair. Maybe he's appointed himself official greeter to all-comers. He looks to be anywhere between six and ten. He's coughing hard and often into a bunch of tissues. The sound seems to come from deep down in his barrel-like chest. He takes a pause from his hacking to look the two of us over.

"Hi, Timmy," Raig greets him. "This is Ellen. She's another student who's working with me like Jonah, and she wants to be a doctor. Good choice of career, eh? Will you look after her, tell her about yourself, while I catch up on some stuff?"

"Sure thing, Raig." Tim grins at me as Raig takes off.

"CF, I've got," he announces. "Have you heard of it?"

The only person I've met with CF is Therese's buddy Jackie, and I've heard very little about it in lectures.

"Yes. Jonah talked to me a bit about you. But I don't know too much about cystic fibrosis. I'm hoping you can teach me. Is there a good place to sit and chat?"

"Sure thing. I'm s'posed to stay pretty much cooped up in my jail cell, anyway. They just let me out for short spells."

He leads the way down the ward corridor past the nurses' station, exchanging greetings with several nurses on the way. I move to help him with his wheelchair, but he is quick to let me know he can manage fine. I wave to my fellow choir members Amy and Carole who are heading down the other corridor toward the exit. Once Tim and I are in his room, he settles himself on the side of his bed. I pull up a chair.

"Yes, cystic fibrosis," Tim resumes. "Right now I'm in for my antibiotics. I have to stay two weeks each time. Hooked up to this IV line—that's where they put my medicines." He points with his free hand to the bottle of fluid hanging from a portable stand.

"Are the medicines for your chest?"

If my ignorance surprises him, he has the grace to hide it. "Right. All this gunk builds up in my lungs. It's real hard to spit up. Mom gives me my physio at home, which helps a lot, then the nurses do it when I'm in here. Mom gets a break."

"How long have you been getting physio?"

"Oh, ever since I was born almost. I've picked up a few things about what's wrong with me." Tim is the picture of nonchalance. "And my doctors and nurses, they make sure I learn all about it."

"How old are you?"

"Thirteen this month. Small for my age, right? I have to take this enzyme at mealtimes to help me digest my food, otherwise I get the runs something awful. But I still don't absorb my food too well, so I don't grow too much. I'll teach you all about it."

"That'd be great, Tim. Thanks. What do you like to do when you're here in the hospital?"

"Watch movies. Play video games. You want to play something? I've got a stack of games."

"Sure, that'd be good."

Tim produces a PlayStation console from his bedside cupboard.

"That looks like it's on loan from the teen lounge."

"Yup. They won't let me in there, though I'm old enough now. They don't want me catching whatever's going around."

The two of us spend the next hour playing Minecraft and Spider-Man. I'm no match for Tim, but this is exactly the distraction I need.

Ten

When we arrive in the ICU on the fourth morning after Jonah's surgery, there is a powerful looking woman chatting with him. She stands several inches taller than me and dwarfs Ann, who is barely five feet tall.

"Hi. I'm Joan. I've just finished Joe's physiotherapy session. He's a real tryer, this one." She grins at Jonah who is perched on the side of his bed, his left arm lying limply at his side. He is wearing shorts and one of his favourite T-shirts—olive green, with a dark blue image of a moose on it. Or maybe it's a caribou. He manages a lopsided grin at Joan.

"And you're like our soccer coach, putting me through this crazy exercise routine right after breakfast." His voice is still a bit slurred, but it's clear enough to understand easily.

"Well, we can't have you sitting around getting fat," Joan retorts.

"Not too much danger of that. I weighed in at 150 pounds, last time I checked."

"Okay, so I'll be back to work with you some more later. And don't forget—keep flexing and texting with those fingers and imagining you're kicking a soccer ball with your left foot."

Ann and I hug Jonah in turn, taking care not to jog his IV line or go anywhere near the turban-like bandage encasing his head. I haven't let myself conjure up that malevolent monster lurking right underneath. Maybe the surgeon has removed that part of his skull completely. My mind skitters away from the image. As I release my grip on him, I take in the bluish-black swelling around both his eyes. I'm stuck for what to say.

Small talk just isn't going to cut it. Ann seems to sense my difficulty and leads off the conversation.

"It's great to see you sitting up and chatting, Jonah. How's your head feeling?"

"Okay, I guess. They're still giving me strong pain meds, but they'll be cutting them back pretty soon. They're making me dozy and like I can hardly get my head around what I want to say."

"Dr. El Khouri told us if this thing had been on the other side of your brain, you might not have been able to talk at all. That's a pretty big blessing."

"Yeah. He was in last night, told me a bit more about what's taken up occupancy in there. I didn't take too much in, but he gave me some literature to read. It's on the table over there."

Ann picks it up and starts to read out loud, then thinks better of it. None of us is ready to hear too much yet. I'm only now starting to get my mind in gear. Doctors must meet patients like Jonah every day and not be totally numbed out. I've got to get my emotions under control, start thinking clearly if I'm going to be any earthly use to Jonah. I pick up the pamphlets Ann has laid on the bed.

"Can I take these, Jonah? We can maybe read them ourselves, then go over them with you later, okay?"

"Sure. I don't need to hear any more right now. All I know is, I'm going to fight this thing. And I'm going to beat it."

He looks steadily at each of us in turn. Moisture gathers on my eyelids. I swallow, rub my fingers over my temples, make no attempt to answer. All I want to do is climb into Jonah's bed and wrap myself around him. Which is not about to happen.

"Oh, and a lady from radiotherapy was in earlier," he goes on. "She says she plans to start treatment in the next little while. I wrote her number down if you want to talk to her."

"Thanks, Joey," his mom says. "We'll maybe do that later. Right now, you look like you're ready to sleep some more."

Jonah wraps his good arm around me and pulls me in close. He whispers, "I love you too."

My heart flips. He must have caught the words I'd murmured as I lay against his chest the night before his surgery.

"Are you ready to look at this stuff?" I ask Ann as we wait for the elevator. "Maybe we could head for the cafeteria and go over it with a couple of strong cups of coffee to fortify us."

"Good plan. I need to know everything about it. We both do—and it'll probably make more sense to you than me."

"This isn't anything I've had lectures about," I tell her. "Let alone encountered on the wards. But since Jonah's not ready to learn too much, I've got to get a clear picture of this thing sitting in his head. And do everything in me to help get rid of it for good."

Ann finds us a table in the corner of the cafeteria while I fetch large lattes and a massive fruit explosion muffin. "That monster is easily big enough for the two of us," Ann says as I take a seat across from her and set the muffin down between us.

I promptly burst into tears, and within a minute or two start laughing, causing a few people to glance briefly our way. Visible displays of emotion are probably common enough around here.

"I don't know what brought that on," I say to Ann after blowing my nose on an assortment of grubby tissues from my jeans pocket. "I guess 'cause you're being so sweet to me. And you've got to be hurting badly yourself."

"Tears are good. Especially right now. I wish I could cry too. I just keep thinking I need to be strong for Joey. And Belinda and Sophie, too. The two of them are very close. Belinda and I were talking most of the night. She's going to stay home with Sophie for the moment. They'll maybe come up on the weekend."

"Well, don't mind me," I answer. "I've always been a crybaby. I'll be fine just as long as I can have a good bawl whenever I need to. It helps me keep my head on straight."

When I take out the pamphlets Jonah has given me, Ann moves around to my side and we read them together. The first thing we see are the two words someone—probably Dr. El Khouri—has printed in black ink at the top: *Anaplastic Astrocytoma.*

"I hope the rest of this is in layman's language," Ann comments. She starts reading it quietly aloud while I listen in.

"A brain tumour is a mass or growth of abnormal cells in your brain. There are many different types. Some are noncancerous (benign) and some are cancerous (malignant). They can begin in your brain (primary) or start in another part of your body and spread to your brain (secondary, or metastatic)."

She pauses to glance up at me. "Jeez, that's even more scary. To think there might be some other cancer in his body, and now it's gone to his brain."

"I'm sure the surgeon would have told us right away if he had any suspicion of that," I say, to reassure myself as much as Ann. "This thing started out in Jonah's brain, not anywhere else."

"Yes, I'm sure you're right."

"And look here," I've scanned down a couple of paragraphs. "Where it lists the different types. Astrocytoma's up at the top, right after acoustic neuroma."

"I wonder what *anaplastic* means."

"It's pretty much the same as malignant," I tell her. "But it has something to do with what they see in the pathology lab."

Ann goes on reading. "Symptoms. These may include headaches, nausea or vomiting, blurred or double vision, loss of sensation or movement in an arm or leg, speech problems, behaviour changes, seizures."

The list goes on longer, but it more or less repeats what we've just read. Ann turns the page to where it goes into more detail about the different kinds of brain tumour. The word *glioma* appears right at the top. There are apparently several different types, but astrocytoma jumps out at us.

"Glioma is what the surgeon called it when he first talked to us," I recall, amazed I can remember a single word from that first conversation. "Astrocytoma must be some form of that. Okay, let's get to what it says about treatment."

We flip through a lot of stuff about risk factors on the third page—things like chemical or radiation exposure and a prior family history.

"I'm quite sure none of these apply to Jonah," Ann says.

Next comes a page about the necessary exams and tests he will need. We finally come to types of treatment on the fifth page of the pamphlet. I offer to take over reading. The words have a dry emotionless feeling.

"Treatment depends on the sort of brain tumour you have, as well as its size and location," I read, keeping my voice quiet. "The most common type of treatment is surgery. The goal is to remove as much of the tumour as possible without damaging the healthy parts of the brain. While some tumours can be removed easily and safely, others may be in an area that limits how much can be removed. But even partial removal of a brain cancer can be beneficial."

I pause to look at Ann. "Well, that's something positive. Even though Dr. El Khouri couldn't remove it all, he said he'd got the bulk of it, and so far, Jonah is making a great recovery." Maybe I'm grasping at straws, but that's exactly what I need to do right now. I go on reading.

"Surgery can be combined with other treatments, which might include radiation and chemotherapy. Physical therapy, occupational therapy, and speech therapy can all help you recover after neurosurgery."

Ann lays her hand on my arm. "This is a lot to take in. I think maybe that's enough for right now." I can tell she's having as hard a time as I am myself.

"Yeah, I certainly don't need to hear any more for the moment."

I pull off a chunk of the muffin that is sitting untouched on the paper plate in front of us. Swallowing it feels like I'm stuffing down feelings that want to jump right out of me. Like I might start screaming my fear and anger at the uncaring universe.

"I bet we could find plenty more detailed stuff on the Internet," says Ann. "But I don't think either of us wants to go there right now any more than Joey does. And it's not always reliable anyway. It's really good doing this together, though."

She wraps her arm around my shoulders and we sit quietly together, oblivious to the comings and goings around us. I lean in against her and close my eyes for a long moment.

"You finish up your half of the muffin," I say at last, nudging it towards Ann. "That piece I ate seems to have got stuck in my throat."

Eleven

Five days after his surgery Jonah is up on crutches. He's still shaky and very much favouring his right side, but they've cut back on his pain meds and he's more awake. Dr. El Khouri has taken his first look at the operation site and pronounced it healing nicely. He has removed some of the surgical clips and replaced Jonah's heavy initial bandage with a much lighter strapping.

An hour later Jonah texts me. "Guess where I am—back on home soil. Just saw Bill heading to the teen room with his guitar. Said he'd drop by in a few and give me a tune or two. Guess I won't be visiting any patient buddies for a while, though. Where are you?"

"Right across the way," I text back. "Tim and I have a game going, but I'm no match for him."

"Tell me about it! I never won a game off him. Can you break away? I'm still doing a whole lot of snoozing, but I want a hug and a kiss first so I'll have sweet dreams."

"On my way," I text back. I high-five Tim, promising I'll be back soon, and head to Jonah's new room. I'm happy to find they have put him in a room on his own. Then it hits me: Jonah has joined a new club: the cancer club. They've put him in isolation because of the heavy therapy they are about to dish out to him. Just like all those other patients with cancer I've come to know. And just like them, before long Jonah will be open to catching all those drug-resistant bugs hospitals seemed to be plagued with. Does that mean it will be family only and I won't be able to see him? I quickly dismiss the thought.

"Hey, your black eyes are fading nicely," I say, trying for a cheery note as I wrap my arms around my boyfriend. I pull my mask down and add a tender lingering kiss. One thing about being in a private room: privacy! I seat myself as close as I can to the top end of his bed, then realize I'm on his left side nearest the door—the side he barely has use of. Jonah manages to bring his right arm over to run his fingers through my curls and stroke my cheek. I pull my mask down to kiss the tips of his fingers.

"Your new head gear looks good, too. Do you have any hair left under there?"

"Nope. I told Dr. El Khouri to shave it all off. I'd have been bald on only one side otherwise. And if I'm being lined up for the same treatment they dish out to some of our patient buddies—well, I'd soon be bald as a billiard ball, anyway."

"What's a billiard ball?"

"Like a pool ball. It just sounds better. British."

I find it in me to smile, but Jonah's words reinforce the reality. He has crossed over this invisible divide. The divide between "us" and "them." I can no longer think of Jonah as a dedicated *care giver*; overnight he's become a totally dependent *care receiver*. Where does that leave me? Have I crossed over with him to the "them" side? Or am I still on the healthy "us" side? What I feel is that I'm smack in the middle between the two. Being swept out of control down a torrential river, with no bank to reach out and hang onto.

"Oh, Jonah, it's so hard to think about this stuff. Maybe it would have been easier if we had never met any of those cancer patients."

"I told you, Ellen, I'm going to beat this thing. Whatever it takes. And I'm still going to graduate in May. Dr. El Khouri has talked to the other specialists—the pediatric oncology team. Even though I'm an adult, he said he usually has the pediatric docs see us students. That's why I'm down here on the peds floor."

"And I'm going to help you, Jonah. With everything I have in me."

I lean forward to bring my lips close against his face again. I inhale the fresh scent of his skin through the fuzz of beard starting to sprout on his chin and cheeks.

"You smell like you just got out of the bath."

"Blanket bath, they call it. My last nurse up in intensive care, Trisha, bathed me just before they moved me down here. Forget personal privacy —that's hospitals for you, I guess. She stripped me down to the buff, though she did have the grace to cover some parts of me"—he nods in the direction of his groin—"with this nice warm towel beforehand. Then she went over me tip to toe with a big warm basin of water. Just worked her way down me on each side—soap, rinse, then pat dry with the towel. Switched to the other side for a repeat performance—soap, rinse, pat. Then she changed the water and washed my buttocks and balls. Told me this was real important, because those were the parts where the skin breaks down and infection gets in most often. Then she rubbed lotion all over me. Well, almost every-where—she drew the line at the covered-up bits! That's why I smell like a newborn baby."

We both giggle. "Well, if you're very good, I'll give you your next blanket bath. And I won't stop short of those bits!"

Now we're guffawing at the daring image I've conjured up. I feel a blush rise in my cheeks. Jonah moves the conversation along.

"I think they'll let me shower pretty soon. As long as I keep my head covered."

We chat for several more minutes before I see Jonah's eyelids start to droop. He makes an effort to rouse himself, offers his lopsided smile. The left side of his mouth stays almost closed.

"It's okay, Joe. You need your sleep, like they told you. I'll just sit here quietly and make sure they don't let anything bad happen to you. Maybe I'll sing you a lullaby to send you off into those sweet dreams."

"Mmm, real nice."

Jonah drifts off as I sing a quiet song or two that we both know, humming the lines I can't recall. I settle myself beside him and think back over our time together. I can still remember my flutters of pleasure when his lips first grazed my cheek, then my lips, his tongue touching mine. We had only started sleeping together regularly in the past month or so. What's this whole catastrophe going to do to our sex life? It isn't too crucial to me, if I'm honest, but I know guys put a lot of store by it—maybe Jonah especially. I've certainly started getting a lot of pleasure out of the sex, and I have the strong sense Jonah can't get enough of it. Hard to talk about that stuff, though—a whole lot easier just to do it.

But this last week has swept all that aside. In its place is my full recognition of my love for this man. It seems to have flowered so swiftly. Is it the knowledge of his cancer, and what this could do to our lives together, that's brought me to this place? This overwhelming love I feel for this suddenly vulnerable boy? Because he no longer seems like a fully grown man to me. And my love has become less a girl–boy passion than one of fierce protection. Almost like Ann must be feeling toward him, mother to son.

I bring my attention back to the hospital room. Fix my gaze on Jonah. While my mind has been running on, his breathing has deepened into slumber. I watch his eyelids flutter, bring my face as close as I can to his, then place a single feather of a kiss on the bruising on his cheek. I reach to grasp his left hand beneath the sheet. The lack of reflex response brings a fullness into my throat. Will he ever be able to wrap this arm tight around me, return the grip of my own hand? At least now COVID's a fading memory I don't have to don gown and mask and gloves to come near him.

I become aware of the room's stillness. Even the drips of fluid into Jonah's IV line from the hanging bag are silent. I want this moment to go on forever. As if I could arrest time. As if I could let my healing love flow into this boy-man in a never-ending stream. To suffuse its power into that malignant thing growing under his skull. Arrest it. Kill it dead forever. Can love really conquer all? Or is that just a Hollywood notion?

I become aware of a bitter fury filling my gut. Speeding up into my chest, flushing through my head, like a furnace ablaze beyond control. Then just as suddenly it has fled up and out of me into the upper recesses of the room. Left in its place is a crushing sadness. I let myself sob in silence as I rest my face against Jonah's shoulder. I'm weeping for the horrible injustice of it all. That this cancer has invaded not only my lover, but his moms, his sister, every one of our Songlines friends who have grown so close.

Perhaps most of all, it has invaded me.

Twelve

The door swings open and Ann is back. Right behind her in the doorway are a man and a woman I haven't seen before. The woman stands a few inches taller than Ann and looks to be in her forties. She's wearing a white coat with a stethoscope slung about her shoulders. The man is older, sixty or so, heavy-set, and balding. Ann smiles at me and moves to the bedside. Jonah stirs and flicks his eyes open, gives me a grin, then takes in his mother and the newcomers.

"Hey, Mom. Must have dropped off. Been doing that a lot."

"How're you doing, sweetheart?"

"I'm okay. My headache's better, and they're cutting back on the pain pills. I managed a BM today. Probably that enema they gave me!" He rolls his head over. "And I've got my girl right here to make sure nothing bad happens to me. She even sang me to sleep."

Ann and I summon smiles, both working to hold back our tears. I can't remember Jonah ever calling me "my girl." Maybe it's his way of introducing me to the new white coats.

"That's good! Well, you've got some visitors. We all arrived together."

The two doctors advance into the room and take up position beside each other at the end of the bed. A united front against the enemy, I let myself hope. The woman speaks to Jonah.

"I'm sorry we've arrived right at the same time as your mom. We rode up in the elevator together, though of course we didn't know each other." She reaches out her right hand to shake Jonah's. "I'm Dr. Kerry Davis. From radiation oncology. Dr. El Khouri asked me to come and see you."

The older man shakes Jonah's hand in turn. "Tom MacIsaac. I'm an oncologist—a cancer specialist. Kerry and I decided it would be best if we came together to talk to you." He pauses and looks inquiringly at me.

"Hi. I'm Ellen, Jonah's girlfriend. You want me to leave?"

"No, no, you're fine," he tells me. "If it's okay with you, Joe. And is it all right if I call you Joe?"

"Joe, Jonah, either one is cool. And yeah, I want Ellen right here. She's heading to medical school next year, so she's our resident expert. She needs to know everything that's going to happen."

Dr. MacIsaac smiles at me. "Then I'm really glad you're on the team."

Ann and I move to perch in the window bay as the doctors pull up chairs and sit on either side of the bed.

"I'm very sorry this has happened to you, Joe," the oncologist starts in. He glances over at Ann. "Should we be waiting for your husband?"

"No, she's at home with our daughter. I'm keeping them both fully up to date with everything that's happening."

There's a brief pause before either of the doctors speak again. Digesting the "she," I guess. Jonah and I haven't talked a lot about his same-sex parents, and I still haven't met his other mom, Belinda.

"Well, as you know, Joe," Dr. MacIsaac resumes, "Dr. El Khouri couldn't cut out the entire tumour."

"Call it cancer, not tumour," Jonah interrupts him. "That's what it is, isn't it? No beating about the bush—this is the real deal."

"Fair enough. Dr. Davis and I are both going to be treating your cancer. We'll be using radiation and drugs in combination. It's going to be tough going for you, but we believe we can beat this thing."

"I'm *going* to beat it," Jonah says at once. "Whatever it takes. But I need you guys in my corner. I know that."

"It's really great to have a fighting attitude—it can make all the difference." Dr. MacIsaac pauses to look over at the other doctor. "We want to get started with your cancer drugs today. Your chemotherapy, that is. And Dr. Davis is planning to begin your radiation in a couple of weeks—once you're fully healed from your surgery." He glances again at his colleague. She is obviously content to let him do the talking. "I've got some forms here that tell you all about it. We can't proceed until you sign them."

"Okay, I'm ready. Where do I sign?"

"Joe, I need to explain things a bit more. Your cancer is rare, and I'm sorry to have to tell you, not everyone makes it. We're always finding new forms of treatment to make things go better. We have this special system for testing new drugs by adding them to our usual ones. It's kind of an experiment, you understand?"

"You mean I'm going to be a guinea pig?"

"No, no, that's not it at all." I catch him glancing over our way, as though checking how we're handling things. I realize my mind is back with the oncologist's reference to a fighting attitude. I've talked a bit to Raig about that idea. How it could make cancer patients feel like it's their fault if the cancer gets the better of them. How they maybe haven't fought hard enough. Raig had agreed. Many children with cancer are living and growing to adulthood, she told me, but by no means all. Is that their own fault? I pull my mind back from this troublesome thought as Dr. MacIsaac goes on talking.

"You see, after surgery, radiation is the standard treatment for a brain cancer, whether or not the surgeon has been able to totally remove it. But now we're finding that some chemotherapy drugs are producing even better results. And most recently medical scientists have discovered your kind of cancer shows certain gene patterns. We're starting to use something we call immunotherapy—a kind of targeted treatment that can kill cancer cells but not healthy cells. All right?"

He pauses to see if any of us want to say anything. Jonah simply nods and no one else speaks.

"Okay, but we haven't been using this new targeted treatment for long enough to be sure if it works or not. And it's just possible it could do more harm than good. Not likely but possible. Joe, we'd like to include you in a national study to try to nail down that answer. If you agree, then we might just give you a chemotherapy drug as well as the radiation treatment. Or we might add another substance—an immune drug—that works to kill the genes on your cancer cells."

There's a brief silence, then Jonah asks, "Okay, so how do you decide?"

"Actually, I don't. It's a computer that does that. We work with a large group of North American cancer centres, with our head office in Toronto. That's where the decisions get made. It's sort of like tossing a coin."

"How do I know if I'm getting this new treatment?"

"That's the thing, Joe, you don't—and nor do I."

"Sounds weird."

"Yeah, I know it does."

"How come you don't get to know?"

"Well, it's about bias. The researchers who thought all this up realized that if we doctors know who's getting the new test drug and who isn't, that could influence the results. We might have our own biases about whether or not the new treatment works. And we might—unconsciously, I should say—let our patients know how we feel about the treatment. Does that make sense?"

"I guess so. Both Ellen and I have taken some psych classes."

"And I've heard about randomized trials," I add. "I think a lot of the pediatric patients are on them."

"Right," the oncologist says. "Most of them, actually. It's the only way we doctors have found to reliably test a promising new treatment. To see if it helps, or conceivably does more harm than good."

"Well, it's your decision, Joe," Ann says after a pause. "But I don't need to hear any more. If your doctors are part of these up-to-the-minute studies to improve things, I'm all for it."

My mind dwells on Dr. MacIsaac's last words. That a new treatment could possibly do more harm than good.

"I understand what you've said about bias," I say. "But what do you mean about the drugs maybe doing more harm? Can you tell us more about that?"

Dr. MacIsaac looks directly at me. I manage to hold his gaze.

"That's a really big question, and I'm glad you asked it. You see, pretty much everything we do in medicine nowadays comes with some sort of risk. Especially with treatments for cancer. Many of the drugs we use have only been around a few years. They have a lot of short-term side effects that we often can't avoid. Like losing your hair and getting low blood counts, those kinds of things. That's why we have these consent forms we need Joe to sign before we go ahead."

He glances down at the papers in his lap, then looks back at Jonah. "But I'm glad to say that most of these side effects are temporary. Your blood counts will recover, your hair will grow back. But I'd be very wrong to state anything for certain. One of the drugs we're planning to use, Joe, has been around for several decades. But early on we found it was causing harm to the muscles of the heart, even in children. Nowadays we give much smaller doses, and we do regular echocardiograms to make sure your heart is beating good and strong. That's just one example. It's very important you all read over these consent forms and make sure you understand them."

There's a longer silence in the room. I feel like this is a real "too much information" moment. How could anyone—anyone without a lifetime's career of studying all this stuff—ever make a fully informed decision? Then it comes to me, the blessed moment of clarity I desperately need.

"I think you mom's absolutely right, Jonah. We have to trust your doctors. I say we read the forms together, ask any more questions that come up, then sign up and go for it."

"Ellen's right on," Jonah says to Dr. MacIsaac. "That's why I have her here working at my side. We'll read everything together, then I'll let you know right away."

"That's great. But I need to go through these forms with you myself, spell out the details, all the things that could happen—good and bad. Then we'll get things running later today if you're all in agreement. But first, it's high time Dr. Davis here got a word in! It's all yours, Kerry."

The radiotherapist uncrosses her legs and takes a moment to look at each of us.

"I'm really glad I was here for this discussion," she starts. "It's not too often I get to sit in on such complex issues. Because I know exactly what treatment I'll be giving you—no tossing of coins! First off, though, we'll be doing what we call a simulation. To make sure we get our radiation treatments right on target and nowhere else, and in the exact right amounts. We'll put little marks on your scalp to guide us each time. We could do that in a few days, Jonah, if you're feeling up to it."

"Am I going to get the drugs and the radiation all at once?"

"Not exactly, no. We're going to wait on our actual radiation treatment for a few weeks. Till you've healed up completely from your surgery. Then we'll only give you the radiation one time."

"You mean it'll all be done in one day?"

"No, no. I mean just one course. Every day for three or four weeks. Weekdays, that is. You see, the radiation goes on killing those cancer cells for a good long time after the treatment is over and done with. And we'll have our own consent forms for you to sign when the time comes."

"What will it feel like?"

"You won't feel a thing. At least, not at the time. You'll probably get really tired, though, and lose your appetite for a few weeks. But that's all." Dr. Davis looks over at us. "Does anyone else have questions for me?"

No one does and she excuses herself.

"Maybe we should all take a short break," Dr. MacIsaac suggests. "Then I'll go over the whole treatment plan and have you sign on the dotted line if you agree."

I glance over at Jonah. He's been pretty quiet, as usual, but I know he's taken in every word the two doctors have said. And I need to be ready to help him think things through so he can make the best decisions, whatever happens down the line.

Thirteen

Jonah is halfway through his first five days of chemotherapy. Dr. MacIsaac has said he plans on giving him six courses altogether. Four of the Songlines choir members show up unannounced at the door of his isolation room: Therese and Dawn, and Jonah's roommates—Bill toting his guitar and Vern holding a bongo drum. They've kept their plans a secret from me as well as Jonah, so it's just the two of us make up the audience. Ann has gone home to spend time with Belinda and Sophie. The choir members are all wearing colourful bandanas as face masks and have donned white coats with stethoscopes draped around their necks. They look like a team of resident doctors making their early-morning rounds.

Jonah rouses up from his doze with a broad, lopsided grin. "Hey, check out those uniforms," he says, giving me a nudge. "Did you lift all that stuff out of some poor intern's locker?"

"No, no," Bill says. "They're just on temporary loan. But maybe we'll need to get our own outfits if we're going to make this a regular gig."

"It's great to see all of you," I tell them. "No big deal with masks and gloves nowadays. But make sure you give your hands a good scrub right now. Don't forget to scrub your nails."

"Yeah, we got strict instructions from the nursing staff," Vern says.

The four of them dutifully wash their hands in the bathroom. I can tell they're nervous about seeing their buddy for the first time since his diagnosis. No doubt wondering how to behave, what to say. But they all look upbeat, and none of them tries to offer Jonah clumsy commiserations.

The great thing is that everyone knows how much good music can be for their fellow choir member.

They break out several favourite tunes, and Dawn takes a couple of solos, Vern banging out a boisterous drumbeat and Bill working up several catchy guitar riffs. It's weird being on the receiving end of all this attention, and I quickly join the performers. It's wonderful to watch Jonah lighting up at the sound of these familiar songs, though it's too much effort for him to join in. Right now, he's meant to be on the receiving end. Vern echoes my thought.

"Just kick back and enjoy, Jonah," he says. "Not often you get to just listen. And we need your expert input to tell us how we're sounding!"

Jonah takes the hint, drops his head back on his pillows, and closes his eyes as we settle into a quieter number. I relish the air of calm spreading through the room and feel a renewed appreciation for just how therapeutic music can be. Jonah has already been experiencing the effects of the chemo—itchy, restless, unable to keep much of anything down. "Awful but get-overable," is how he puts it with his typical reserve. But these joyful sounds and the company of his friends are clearly lifting him out of the blues threatening to beset him.

"That was fantastic, guys," he exclaims as they wrap up. "It's great to hear how your voices blend. Now I know what it's like to be on the receiving end, and it's really given me a big lift. Thanks, all of you."

As soon as his first course of chemo is over and Jonah is starting to recover some of his physical and mental energy, Dr. Davis brings him down to her department for the simulation she's talked about.

"It turned out to be a big deal," Jonah tells me later. "First, the two techs, Betty and Thomas, had to place my body in the exactly right position on this hard bed. Then they put me through their own CAT scanner so they could pinpoint the precise spots for the X-ray beams to target. They have to be certain not to stray one millimetre off target."

"Did they tell you what kind of machine they'll be using?" I ask. "I've read they're developing new machines that deliver different radiation particles."

"Yes, they call it a LINAC—short for linear accelerator. Betty says that's what they mostly use to shoot high-energy electrons at cancers. They marked me up with tattoos to be right on target—not like in a tattoo parlour, though." He grins. "Just tiny indelible punctures in my scalp that will never wash off. You can't see them, they're under the dressing, and they'll be invisible once my hair grows back. The last thing was a special plastic mask they fit on me to keep my head in place. The whole simulation took forever, but they assured me each radiation treatment would only take a few minutes. Monday through Friday for several weeks. I get a break on the weekends."

Jonah does indeed feel absolutely nothing during these treatments. But the combination of the chemo and radiation starts to take its toll. The puking and being unable to eat almost any solid food are the worst, and the effects seem to get worse each day. I arrive each morning to find him exhausted after his early-morning trip to the radiotherapy department. He could go home for a break on the weekends, but the chemo has made his blood counts plummet, and everyone is nervous about him catching a bad infection. That would be disaster in his already weakened state.

Jonah somehow rallies when the physiotherapist shows up to put him through his paces. And I learn the exercises to help strengthen the weak muscles in his arm and leg. Especially all the tiny movements of his fingers, which need the most work. It brings home to me just how much we depend on our hands to get along in the world—office, car, computer, you name it.

Jonah can make it to the bathroom with the help of a four-legged walking frame, while the nurses or I help him with his IV equipment. I hardly admit it to myself, but I come to relish these moments when I can show my love for him through such simple acts. I know Jonah hates his helplessness and I do my best to hold back when he gets mad at himself.

"It took me fifteen minutes to text Vern to bring in some of my clothes," he tells me. "It's driving me crazy!"

I hold back from suggesting I take care of stuff like that. The only time he seems like his old self is when any of the Songlines choir show up to serenade him with favourites from their repertoire. They've got over their nervousness at being with their sick friend, and it becomes a regular event for one or two of them to drop by between classes. They're always scrupulous with handwashing and know to stay a million miles away if anyone feels a cold coming on. Apart from Bill, who is always on guitar, several of us are adept with hand drums, and the others bring rattles. We add in several lively new riffs.

Now mid-terms are behind me, I'm back singing regularly with Songlines. Raig sometimes shows up to conduct us, though we hardly need her. Bill and Vern have both shaved their heads to a shiny baldness in a gesture of support for Jonah. We quickly give up on the white coats and stethoscopes but take to sporting multicolored caps of the kind popular in the operating rooms, in addition to our bandanas. Dawn has worked up some low-key dance moves that she can somehow perform in the doorway.

"We may not be official members of your medical team," Therese tells Jonah at the end of a number, "but we've learned a thing or two about song and dance. It's good for healing whatever needs healing."

"Maybe we should rename ourselves The Songlines Song and Dance Band," Dawn adds as she recovers her breath.

The day after Jonah completes his radiation treatment coincides with the end of his second course of chemo. The whole choir heads to his room to celebrate. The staff nurse promptly rules out our trooping into his room, but she lets us all gather around the open door to perform. Raig has even typed up a program, and we distribute copies to the nurses and many of the patients. We've chosen songs mostly recorded by Atlantic Canadian artists—Joel Plaskett's "Love This Town," Great Big Sea's "Run, Run Away," and Wintersleep's "Forest Fire." Jonah is immediately cheered by the music, but after the fourth number he's starting to drift off. I suggest we cut the celebration short.

Several of the nurses and the more mobile patients have gathered to listen by this time, and they offer tumultuous applause. Jonah rouses himself enough to grin and murmur thanks. I'm doing my best to stem my tears. I have a hard time picturing Jonah ever getting back to his easygoing self. He's lost so much weight, and he gets mad at the efforts of the nurses to get him to eat. Will he ever be part of Songlines again, or get to make visits with his old patient buddies? Get back to school full-time so he can graduate and fulfill his dream of graduate school? I cheer myself by reflecting just how therapeutic music can be in this present moment. The future will just have to take care of itself.

Fourteen

November

During the week after Jonah finishes radiation and his second course of chemo, Dr. MacIsaac orders a repeat of his scans to see how well the treatment's working. He comes by the morning afterwards. I am still making Jonah's room my first port of call for short spells each day. The oncologist always greets me warmly if I'm there, pulls up a chair, and never seems in a hurry to head out. Not like the resident doctors who take care of things day to day. They almost never accompany Dr. MacIsaac when he comes by in the afternoons to talk with Jonah.

"The residents and med students mostly show up when it's still dark in the morning," Jonah tells me. "They use their flashlights to peer at me and ask me a couple of rote questions about how I'm doing. I mumble "no problem" and they take off. I guess that's the life of a medical intern, babe." He grins at me.

"Well, I'd sure try to join my boss whenever he's making his own rounds."

"I know. But I got to talk to a couple of them. It's really true what they say—about eighteen-hour days and stuff."

"Where do they find time to take care of themselves?" I quickly realize there's no good answer to that. I picture being a medical student, then an intern in a few short years. I make a silent pact that I'll try to be present with every patient I have to care for, no matter how busy or exhausted I may be.

"You're making great progress, Joe," Dr. MacIsaac says as soon as he sits down. "Your new scans show the cancer has shrunk a good fifty per cent. It really helps that you're young—you'll soon be getting back to your old self, believe me. Now you've earned yourself a break before going on with more courses of chemo."

"What about the other fifty per cent?" Jonah presses him. "Won't that grow right back if you stop now?"

"No, no. The treatment goes on working, killing off cancer cells as they develop inside you. And we'll be giving you several more courses once your body's had a chance to recover some."

"How do you know when you've given me enough?"

"We won't actually know that for certain, Joe. It's only what happens in the future after we finish your treatment that can tell us that." He leans forward, rests his elbows on his knees. "Let me tell you a story. When I started my training forty years ago, cancer specialists were leery about ever stopping treatment. They couldn't get their heads around the idea. Well, I had this patient with cancer—she was about your age—and she'd been receiving chemo for over three years.

"It was at my very first clinic she told me, 'Enough already—this chemo is messing with my social life. When will I get done with it?' Well, of course I had no idea how to answer her, so I asked the professor I was working for how long he would be continuing. Right off he told me, 'I've never stopped anyone's treatment. But maybe it's time I did. If we haven't cured her yet, I guess we never will.' Well, he stopped her chemo for good that very day. I looked after her the whole three years of my training, and I got to go to her wedding. She's maybe bouncing grandkids on her knee round about now."

The oncologist grins at us both. "You see, that's the only way we'll finally know if we've given you enough treatment—when you have children and maybe grandchildren of your own. Though I don't think I'll be around to meet them!"

Dr. MacIsaac smiles some more, which brings grins from us as we glance shyly at each other. My own smile grows wider at the thought of Jonah and me being grandparents. I feel myself warming to the oncologist as he finishes telling his story. It's lovely that he's willing to share some of his own life. I can tell Jonah is really taken with it too.

When Ann arrives to take him home for the two-week break before his next chemo course, she tells me she wants to get him settled in before she has me join them.

"It's going to be a hard adjustment. Joe's only been home for brief visits over this last year. As you know, he was doing research for his senior thesis most of the summer. And everything that's happened lately has been real, real hard on the rest of the family. I promise I'll call you just as soon as he's settled in. We all want you to come spend a few days—and it will be really good for Joe." Her phone buzzes, and she speaks briefly to the voice at the other end. "The car's waiting downstairs. Can you take Jonah's suitcase and help him into the elevator?"

Belinda is sitting in the driver's seat. Jonah greets her with a long-drawn-out hug, then pulls back to look into her eyes. As he introduces me to her I can see the glisten of unshed tears behind her eyelashes. He turns to embrace me clumsily before easing himself into the back of the car with Ann's help. Belinda stays seated in the driver's seat but summons a smile for me.

"Hello! I hear you're going to come visit soon. I'm looking forward to getting to know you."

I stand watching the car's retreat down the driveway in front of the hospital. I'm already impatient for Jonah's call, most especially for my visit to his home near Port Hawkesbury, almost three hours' drive away.

Fifteen

I have to wait several days, well aware of my promise not to pick up the phone to call or to text. I know it will take a while for Belinda and Sophie to adjust to having him back home. They say absence makes the heart grow fonder. You don't have to tell me.

The first week of Jonah's time at home coincides with fall study break from classes. I spend time hanging out with Timmy, as I've learned to call him, and a few other patients I've come to know, though both Darl and Dylan have gone home. But since Jonah's illness I'm finding the whole hospital environment oppressive. I'll find myself taking in all the sharp angles of the walls in a corridor leading from one department to another. No gentle curves, soft lighting, calming ambient music. I think of the animal scientist Temple Grandin, who showed how cattle moving on curved chutes in slaughterhouses were much calmer because they couldn't see their way ahead. Why can't they build hospitals like that?

I try hitting the books at one of the gleaming pine tables in the university library, but I'm quickly flipping the pages of my biology, physics, and organic chemistry textbooks, barely focusing on either words or images. My mind keeps straying to thoughts of Jonah as I'd last seen him, leaning his weight on his walker almost like an old man, needing our help to stumble into the back of the car. He and I have only been apart for brief spells since our first date. I can instantly hear the rhythms and intonations of his voice, laid-back and thoughtful. Quite unlike the fast-paced joshing most guys adopt, yet he's always alive and infectiously open to everything and everyone. There's barely been any tension between us. Sometimes I wonder if we'll ever find anything to fight about. My throat thickens as I recapture the sensation of our first kiss. It had felt so *safe*. I can still feel the touch of his fingers beneath my elbows.

"You're delicious," he'd murmured, and smiled blissfully. I had found myself gazing at that graceful slope between his nose and his upper lip, then leaning forward to softly return his kiss, right there on that very spot. In my first year of middle school, when I was starting my puberty growth spurt, my breasts had grown so fast I'd become a target for all the boys. As though touching them was like capturing some kind of flag. But Jonah has always been gentle and slow.

He finally phones on Friday afternoon. "You missing me?" His voice is weak, and I have to turn the volume up to catch his words.

"What d'you think? I miss you horribly. When can I come visit?"

"How about tomorrow morning? Catch the early bus, and my mom will pick you up at the station downtown."

"Wonderful! I won't sleep a wink."

I have an immediate flurry of nerves as I climb down from the bus and see Ann standing beside her parked car. How will it be to see Jonah with his family? How is Sophie coping with her big brother's terrible illness? Will she get jealous if he pays me too much attention? And what about Belinda? I've barely spoken to her. All I know is she works for a politician who keeps her travelling for work a lot, even on weekends.

It's Belinda who greets us as Ann pulls up in front of their house. I sense tension in her grip as she shakes hands with me. She offers a brief smile as she reaches into the trunk for my suitcase. I take in her height and the effortless way she handles my luggage. Her face looks devoid of makeup, and there are taut lines around her eyes and mouth. Her greying hair swings loose as she moves back into the house.

"Jonah's still sleeping—or he was when I last checked," she says. "But he wanted to see you as soon as you got here."

Ann disappears into the kitchen and Belinda leads me upstairs, still holding my case. She leaves it at the top of the stairs, then moves on down the short passageway to knock on a door at the end.

"Come on in," comes Jonah's quiet voice.

He's sitting up in bed wearing one of my favourite shirts, the olive-green tee with a rose-coloured image of a heart. It always looks anatomically correct to me: a living lesson in anatomy. Belinda moves to the bedside and hugs him briefly, then turns back to me standing in the doorway.

"I'm going to leave you two to catch up, then I'll bring you a cup of tea."

"No need, Mom, I'm going to get up in a few," Jonah answers as I clear off clothes and magazines from the chair by his bed and sit down. As soon as Belinda closes the door, I get up again and reach in to wrap my arms about him. There's still minimal movement of his left side, but I hold back from commenting. Time enough when I've got over my unfamiliar shyness. I finally loosen my arms from around his neck and plant a long kiss on his lips.

"I've missed you, babe," he tells me as I break away.

"I've missed *you*. No early morning kisses and cuddles for almost a week. I could hardly stand it!"

"It's awesome to have you here at last. I'm not letting you run right back to school. I need you to nurse me better!"

I grin at him and lean in for another kiss. "I'm so happy I'm here, but I feel pretty shy around Belinda. Is she okay with me visiting like this? She must be having a real hard time with what's happening to you. And I've hardly met her. Not like Ann, we were almost in each other's pockets the first couple of weeks after you got sick."

"Yeah, they're very different, my moms. Opposites attract, eh?"

"We haven't talked much about your family," I say as I sit back down. "Is there a dad in the picture? I mean, am I going to be meeting him too?"

"Unlikely any time soon. Sure there's a dad, but I haven't met him myself yet."

"Yet?"

"Well, he's not exactly anonymous. In fact, you can't be an anonymous sperm donor anymore. He got in touch with me last year, but we still haven't met."

"Which one's your biological mom?"

"Ann is."

"And what does that make Belinda?"

"My other mom! And she's Sophie's too."

"They're married, right?"

"Twenty-plus years. They decided pretty early on they wanted to have kids. And it turned out Ann was the best one to carry us both. She's eight years younger than Belinda."

"Does Sophie have the same dad?"

"No, no. We're half-siblings. She can expect to hear from her own dad sometime after she turns eighteen. There's a whole lot of us half-sibs around nowadays. They say some sperm donors have fathered a bunch of children. My dad told me he's happily married, but his wife is infertile. His name's Ethan, by the way, and he's the same age as Belinda—forty-eight. Anyway, his wife gave her blessing to his registering with the cryobank in Alberta. That's where they live. I could have a bunch of half-siblings for all I know—and I guess I could find out in time."

"D'you know other guys like you, with two moms?"

"Sure, yeah. My moms always went to LGBTQ support groups and usually took me along. I was pretty much raised in the gay community. But I definitely like girls best, in case you had doubts!"

We grin at each other, and I decide this is a good moment to check things out some more. I move in close, and he shifts over to make room on the bed so I can bring my legs up. The kiss goes on long enough for me to feel the surge deep in my pelvis that I'd almost forgotten. I cling onto him, swept up in a mix of happiness and fear. Fear that all this joy could be quickly swept out of our lives. I try to push down the shadowy feelings within me as I break away.

"We should go down and check on them. Here I am, their brand-new house guest, and I've vanished straight into their son's bedroom. They'll be thinking we're getting it on already!"

"Oh, they'd be cool with it. They know how I feel about you." He places a kiss on the tip of my nose as he unwinds himself from me. "But you're right, it's high time we put in an appearance. Sophie's been hearing a lot about you. I know she wants to see whether you live up to her expectations."

Another thought strikes me. "You call both of them Mom, right? Not by their first names or anything?"

"Yes. They've often told me to use their first names, especially lately. But I'm just sticking to 'Mom' right now. I like the power it gives me—when we're all sitting around the kitchen table, they don't know which of them I'm talking to. Hilarious."

"Well, it's pretty clear in our house which parent I'm talking to!"

"Hey, it's high time I met your folks. I know it's harder, with them being two provinces away. Must be a long drive. You can get there by train though, can't you?"

"It means changing in Montreal. But yeah, you're right. Mom says they really want to meet you. We need to set it up—maybe even for Christmas. What do you think?"

"Sounds like a plan. My moms might not be too crazy about not having me home for Christmas, though. Nor Sophie."

Jonah swings both legs over the side of the bed and reaches for the walker leaning against the bedpost. I quickly move to help him.

"No, I'm good, I'm getting the hang of this. And I'm feeling some of my strength coming back. My balance too—thanks to all those exercises the physiotherapist taught me. I might need a bit of help zipping up my jeans, though."

The jeans are lying on the end of the bed, and he starts hauling them over his black boxers while I'm still sitting beside him. I hold back, sensing he wants to do as much as he can himself. He swings his legs over the side and lets me hoist them over his butt and help with the zipper and button at the front. We've seen each naked before, but this is a first—zipping my boyfriend's pants up. I feel my heart open wide. How long will he need help with simple stuff like this? Whatever, I'm going to be there for him.

I hold the door open as he makes his way out into the corridor, grasping the walker and swinging his left leg to the side as he moves forward. Ann comes out from the kitchen as she hears us come downstairs.

"You making it okay, you two?"

"Yup, I've got some good help here," Jonah says as he hangs onto the banister with his good hand. Sensing he doesn't want help, I watch from two steps below as he hops down each step on his right leg, then swings his left one down to join it. I'm ready to applaud.

"Gripping onto something solid like the banister is a big help," he tells me as he descends.

I'm inhaling the delicious aroma of baking from the kitchen long before we reach the bottom step. The rest of the family is gathered around the kitchen table, nursing large mugs of coffee and nibbling an assortment of what look like homemade muffins. Sophie is at the head of the table, dressed in striped sweater and jeans, dark brown hair swept back in a ponytail. She smiles shyly at me without getting up.

"It's great to finally meet you, Sophie," I say, grinning back. "Your brother's been telling me wonderful things about you." I pause. "I'm sorry he's having such a hard time right now."

There's silence around the table, and I think for a moment Sophie is going to lose it. Was it a dreadful mistake to bring up Jonah's illness right after we've just met? Jonah quickly intervenes.

"I'm making it, right, Sis?" He wraps his good arm around Sophie's shoulders. "With a whole lot of help from you, I might say."

Sophie manages another smile and pulls out the chair beside her.

"You sit here, Ellen," Ann says, indicating the empty seat at the other end of the table. "I'll get you a coffee. Milk, no sugar, right?"

"Right."

Belinda smiles at me. "There's one blueberry muffin left, otherwise I think it's banana nut."

I tear off half the blueberry muffin. "Half for you, Jonah." I take a big bite of my own half. Still warm and utterly delicious.

"Who baked these? I never tasted a muffin this good."

"That would be me," Ann says.

"Mom's a professional," Jonah tells me. "Really. She bakes for a living—and we're the lucky people she tries out her new creations on."

"That's right," Belinda adds. "Me, I just trot off to the office every day like the rest of the working stiffs."

"You work for a politician, don't you?" I ask her.

"Yes, our local MLA. All kinds of constituency and party caucus stuff. She keeps me hopping."

"That office would cease running altogether without our Belinda," Ann says, smiling at her spouse.

"And this household would starve without you," Belinda responds. "As would a bunch of other households. I long ago lost count of how many get all their bread and other baked goodies from you."

I catch the loving look that passes between the two of them. Are they husband and wife? Spouses? I wonder what the politically correct term is for same-sex partners nowadays?

"You do all your sales right here?" I ask Ann.

"Yes, and at our farmer's market. Wednesdays and Saturdays, that is. One of the family comes along to help out on Saturdays, which is a lot busier. A friend is mostly there with me on Wednesdays."

"I guess things must have ground to a halt while you were at the hospital."

"Yeah, it didn't take long for the word to get out. Jonah's got our whole neighborhood rooting for him!"

I had planned to only stay for the weekend, but the family won't hear of it.

"Joey tells me you're still not taking your full load of classes, right?" Ann says as soon as I ask her about the Sunday bus schedule. "And Joe's got all his textbooks with him. He's still determined to graduate at the end of this school year, and I know some of your coursework overlaps. How about the two of you study in the mornings, then you can help me out with our bees in the afternoon while Jonah's taking his nap."

"Wow, bees—I want to know more about that!" I answer. "And you're right, my dean says it's fine if I do my classes online instead of in person."

"Then that's settled."

"Thanks for making me so welcome. And it's a great idea about us studying together. We've done a good bit of that." I smile at her. "But I've never had anything to do with bees. Don't you get stung a lot?"

"Not once you know what you're doing. Don't worry, I'll show you—it's a whole lot of fun."

The late fall weather is warmer than usual, and the backyard is still partly hidden from the house by maples and oaks in their fall glory. But as I look out the kitchen window, I can see several rectangular constructions perched on the grass beyond the trees. They have to be the beehives.

"That sounds cool. I've always wanted to learn more about bees. I only know how important they are to the ecosystem, not too much more. I'll try not to get in your way."

Sixteen

I hear the car take off as I stir from a restful sleep on Monday morning. I check my watch: ten to eight. Belinda's told me she always drops Sophie off at school before heading to the office. I know Jonah will still be asleep, so I head for the bathroom, then pull on my clothes and head downstairs. I am greeted once more by the smell of baking as Ann meets me with a mug of coffee in the same ceramic mug as yesterday. The paintwork on it looks like the work of a young child—bright blue mingled with small pink hearts. Sophie's or Jonah's handiwork, no doubt.

"I changed my mind about waiting till the afternoon to tend to the bees. It's pretty warm right now, but who knows how long that will last. I thought we could head out right after breakfast, and I'll introduce you to my other family. There are still some honeycombs left to collect. Then Jonah should be up and ready for your session."

After waffles topped with scrambled eggs and homemade salsa, Ann leads me up the yard to a small shed. She hands me a long white coat, veil, and gloves.

"The first task is to get my smoker going." She takes a metal canister off the shelf and stuffs it with newspaper. "This is what I use first, then I add small bits of kindling and pine needles. I always keep a store of them handy."

She uses the small leather bellows attached to the side of the canister to drive smoke out of the spout at the top. It takes several minutes before the smoke is flowing evenly, then we set off through the trees to the small cluster of hives. Despite Ann's reassurance, I feel a flutter of nerves as we approach. She reads my mind.

"They do sting, sure, but not too often. And only if you don't know how to approach them. Mostly, they hardly know you're there."

She reaches the first of the six hives and lifts the cover, then uses the bellows to direct the smoke downwards into the hive. "The theory is the smoke calms them down, but some say it gives them the idea there's a fire nearby. Which makes them focus on stuffing themselves with honey, so they're all set for flight if need be. That's what most experts have decided, anyway."

There are very few bees in sight at the top of the hive. "Where are they all?"

"They drop down to the bottom level during the night. It's good to check on them early in the morning—easier. The season is just now finishing," she adds, "so I'll need to add artificial feed."

"What do you mean, artificial?"

"Well, there's not much pollen or nectar around anymore, which means I need to feed each hive with granulated sugar and water. It nourishes them for their winter hibernation. The beekeeper who taught me showed me a simple way to do it. I use a zip-lock baggie almost full of the syrup I've made up from cane sugar and water. Good way to recycle them. I cut two or three slits so the bees can easily slurp it up."

"Cool! Will we see any queens?"

"Probably not. She mostly hangs out in the brood chamber, right below these storage sections." Ann points to the row of frames below the cover. "That's where she spends most of her life. She can lay up to three thousand eggs a day—if the worker bees have done their job of feeding her and keeping her happy. I have a few queens who survived from last year, but it's always touch and go. I often have to replace several that have died."

"There are different kinds of bees, right?"

"Right. These are Italian. A lot of beekeepers around here use them. They're nice and gentle, and they do well through the winter. We don't get our first honey flowing till late June." Ann is leading me between the hives as we talk, applying the bellows to the top of each one. "It's pretty sheltered here, so the bees winter well if the weather's not too harsh. I always lose more than I'd like to, though. I keep a couple of hives empty in spring in case some of the bees swarm and are looking for a new home."

We move slowly from hive to hive and repeat the process of smoking, inspecting, and feeding the bees with Ann's syrup at each one. She lets me take over for the last couple of hives. I feel the comfort of her guidance and companionship as I carry out these tranquil tasks. As we finish up, we hear Jonah open the door from the kitchen onto the porch.

"Looks like you're making yourself useful out there, babe!"

"You bet," I call back. "And I guess you didn't need any help getting yourself up and about."

"Nope. Just took my time. I'm getting stronger every day."

"We're almost done," Ann tells him. "You fixed yourself some coffee?"

"Yeah, I'm fine. No worries."

Minutes later I finish working on the last hive with Ann looking on. We store all the equipment back in the garden shed and join Jonah on the porch. He's put on a sweater, even though it's still warm. He seems to feel the chill a lot more than before he got sick.

"That was a lot of fun," I say, sitting in the wicker chair beside him. "I was nervous at first, but I had no idea how easy and peaceable it would be. I could do this for a living!"

"Pretty tough making it a full-time occupation," Ann says. "And as you can see, there's a good bit of work involved. But you're right, it's a wonderful pastime. And I sell a fair bit of honey at the market—along with my baked goodies and beeswax candles. We'll head over there on Wednesday."

"That would be great," I say, choosing not to mention that this is turning into a very long weekend visit.

"Now, on a completely different topic," Ann says, grinning broadly at us both. "There's no reason you have to sleep in the spare room, Ellen—unless you prefer it, of course. As I'm sure you noticed, it's really our box room, so there's hardly space to swing a cat."

Jonah and I glance at each other shyly, and I can't help giggling.

"Well, if you don't think Sophie will mind. I mean, I don't want to shock her!"

"Sophie's pretty possessive of her big brother, but she knows you two are very close. She'll be fine with it."

"Thanks, Mom," Jonah says. "I felt mighty lonely the last two nights with Ellen right next door."

We all laugh, though I sense the unspoken thought between us. How many nights will we get to spend together in the near future? Thank goodness Ann didn't feel the need to talk about taking precautions.

Seventeen

Jonah still tires after being up only a few hours. The radiation therapist, Dr. Davis, had told us the effects of her therapy could last several weeks, so we attribute it mostly to this. And combining it with several rounds of chemo surely doesn't help. But it gives us a good excuse to head up to bed right after supper that night. I feel a brief attack of nerves—it's been almost two months since the two of us slept in the same bed. I'm not at all sure what effect Jonah's cancer or its treatment has had on his sex drive. Will I have to be the one to take the initiative?

As we cuddle up in Jonah's bed, I'm inhibited by the thought of the rest of his family very much awake right below us. We lie quietly side by side, listening in the dark to the quiet voices downstairs. We hear Sophie say night-night to Ann and Belinda, then head up to the bathroom before her bedroom door closes. Within a few minutes the two moms follow suit, and the house falls silent. I envision them settling down for the night at the far end of the passage. I can tell Jonah is still awake beside me. Is he worried I'm looking for a show of unbridled passion after this lengthy spell of abstinence? No time like the present to find out. I roll my body against his and start to stroke his face and chest, taking things slowly and not breaking the silence. After several minutes I take his good hand and lay it over my breasts. I sense his anxiety. Is he worried about whether he can perform to my satisfaction? His murmured words confirm what's going on with him.

"Oh God, I want you, Ellen," he whispers. "It's just…I don't know if I can, you know…"

"Babe, we don't have to do anything. I just love being close to you. I've missed it so much. I don't need anything more. I just love your mom giving us the okay to share your bed."

I reach over to his left hand and stroke it. "Is the feeling coming back in your hand at all?"

"Yeah, some, I think. It's kind of tickly when you stroke it."

I let my hand run down his left side to his thigh. "How about down here?"

"Yeah, I don't think it's numb down there." He moves my hand over to his groin and between his legs. "Not much happening in this department, though, right? I've tried a few times, but I can't seem to get it up."

"It's okay, babe. I'll bet it's just temporary. You've been through a whole lot. But there wasn't anything in the stuff I read about not being able to have sex after radiation or chemo."

"Ah! You've been reading up about it, have you?" I sense Jonah grinning in the dark.

"Sure I have. Hey, I'm pretty curious, you know!"

"Well, I like having your body right here beside me, that's for sure. You feel good."

"You do, too. I guess we'll just have to be patient for a while. Probably doesn't help to have your moms only a few feet away. You maybe don't make a habit of bringing girls home to sleep with you?"

"You've got that right. You're the first, babe. And the last, I hope."

His voice trails off. Perhaps he's caught the unintended suggestion in his words. We lie silent once more, then I resume stroking him between his legs. I reach to take his penis in my hand.

"Hmm, that feels good, I've got to say." Jonah turns to kiss my lips, then my neck and collar bone. I can feel the stirring as I continue the gentle strokes of my hand.

"Hey, it just could be you're starting to get sensation back."

"I think maybe you're right. Don't stop now, okay?"

I become aware of my own wetness and draw Jonah's good hand down my belly from my breast.

"Ah, now that feels good too."

"It doesn't seem like you've lost any of *your* sex drive," Jonah whispers.

"Guess not. Just carry right on—but if you fall asleep it'll be okay too. I'll still love you."

As Jonah's right hand continues to move gently between my legs, I close my eyes and snuggle up against his side. The last thought I have before I drift off to sleep is that my own hand is tiring from its rhythmic movement. And that Jonah's strokes are slowly subsiding. When I open my eyes again, the early morning sunlight is filtering through the curtains. We cuddle together, kiss our good mornings, and become aware of sounds coming up from the kitchen.

"Any dreams?" I ask Jonah.

"Not wet ones anyway. No, I guess my sleep was pretty dreamless."

"Me too. It felt lovely."

The next few days pass quickly and joyfully. Jonah and I put in a couple of hours working on our laptops each morning. It proves great therapy for his hand and finger movements. We explore the neighbourhood after his afternoon naps, with Jonah managing slightly longer distances each time. The university and schoolwork have receded in my mind, and I find myself relishing the slow pace of our days. Therese and I have texted back and forth several times. Vern has been staying over at our place and all the Songlines members send their greetings.

"Vern says to not hurry back," Therese texts. "He likes having the apartment just for the two of us."

Friday morning, Jonah gets the call from the oncologist's office we'd been trying to push out of our minds. Time for his next round of chemo. Dr. MacIsaac had warned us all before Jonah left the hospital that he'd be stepping up the intensity now that he was through with his radiation. The resident doctor tells him on the phone that they'll have a bed ready for him on Monday.

"How long will I be staying this time?" Jonah asks her.

"I'm not sure. You'll have to ask Dr. MacIsaac when you see him. But I know he wants you to get several rounds of chemotherapy in as short a time as possible."

Ann and I accompany Jonah back to the hospital. It proves a whole lot harder checking back in after his two-week break. But at least Jonah has his appetite back and has regained some of the weight he lost over the surgery and the first two rounds of chemo. And he's happy to see a few familiar faces among the nurses. Dr. MacIsaac comes by to check him out Monday afternoon. Ann and I had been about to leave, but he encourages us to stay.

"Good to have you both here. Joe needs all the support he can get. And one of you can stay overnight again—or take it in turns if that works out better." He turns his attention to Jonah to put him through his physical exam. "You've certainly got a bit more strength in that left side, Joe, which is a very good sign. And I'll have the physio team working with you again while you're here."

"How long are you going to keep me in this time?"

"That all depends on how you handle the chemo. Your white blood count will dip low again, which will leave you open to those nasty infections that thrive in hospitals. What's the driving time to where you live?"

"It's about three hours by car. But I saw Dr. Goldmann, my family doctor, while I was home, so she knows what's going on. She says she can see me any time if I have problems."

"Yeah, I've talked to her too. She trained here, so she's looked after a few cancer patients and will know what to look out for. But no promises. It's important we get you through the rest of the chemo as fast as we can, so the cancer doesn't start growing back."

I pose the question I sense Jonah and Ann are scared to ask. "How often does that happen?"

Dr. MacIsaac looks at me as though making up his mind how to respond. Then answers with his own question.

"Have you been reading up on Jonah's condition? You're hoping to go to med school, so I expect you've doing your own research?"

I know my discomfort shows in my face. "Yes. I've been reading what I can find, not just the literature you and Dr. El Khouri gave us. But I haven't talked too much about it." I glance quickly at Ann and Jonah. "I'm sorry, guys. I just felt I had to know everything I could, but that you two had all the info you needed already. And Sophie and Belinda, for sure."

There is silence, but not an awkward one. I feel relief at having fessed up—maybe they aren't too mad at me.

"Makes sense to me," Dr. MacIsaac says at last. "It's good to have one person wanting to get the full scoop—and you're the obvious one, given your career plans. Well, as you know, Jonah's cancer wasn't totally operable." He turns his attention to his patient. "But the best-case scenario now is if it shrinks down enough for Dr. El Khouri to go back in and cut the rest out.

Without doing any more harm to the rest of your nervous system, that is. It's a real possibility. And like I said before, your age is on your side." He grins briefly. "I know you're a fully grown man now, Joe, but you're still very much a kid to me. And you young guys can handle chemo a whole lot better than I could in your situation."

I sense the oncologist isn't about to offer a definitive answer to my question. Well, maybe I don't want to hear more statistics. I remember my research professor telling me reading a statistical chart is like looking at a mountain through a tennis racket: you can see pretty much whatever you want to see.

I exchange a smile with Jonah and squeeze his hand.

Eighteen

December

I meet up with Raig to bring her up to date. I tell her I'm ready to spend some time with my patient buddies again.

"I guess Jonah must be feeling like family to you nowadays, eh?"

"He does, Raig. And the rest of his family is getting to be that way too. They made me totally at home while I was there. And Ann—Jonah's mom—had me help with her beehives. The best kind of therapy I could dream of."

"I'm so glad. Well, your buddy Timmy has just gone home, but Darl is back in for her regular transfusion, and she's pretty down in the dumps. D'you think you're up for visiting her?"

"Yes. It'll get my mind off my own worries. And I always learn a lot I'd never get in class."

I find Darl in the adolescent bay, sitting up with a laptop balanced on her knees.

"I'm trying to keep up with my schoolwork," she tells me when I ask her what she's into. "I'm due to graduate high school this spring, and I don't want to have to repeat a semester—or more."

"Well, I'm not that long out of high school," I tell her, "so maybe I can help. If I had any of the courses you're taking, that is. What are you studying?"

"The science courses are the toughest ones for me. I could never work up much interest in physics and chemistry and stuff. But I found out most universities expect you to have at least three years of science credits. I'm doing my best to catch up."

"What are you planning to do after school?" I ask.

"I want to be a social worker, like my mom," Darl answers promptly. "But I never thought I would need this much science."

"That's what my dad does. Out in our small community, mostly—and you're right, he never seems to bring much science to his work. He's just a lovely people person. But me, I'm pretty much a science nerd, so maybe I can help you out after a bit."

"What about you? What are you planning to do?" Darl asks as I pull a chair close to the bedside. "I mean, once you get done with university?"

"I'm hoping to get into medical school. But it's very competitive."

"How come you've got time to hang out with folks like me? Don't you have a bunch of classes to go to?"

"Well, it turns out most med schools encourage applicants to get as much hands-on experience as we can. Which means spending time with patients like you, not just hitting the books." I pause, then decide to keep going. "And right now I'm taking a couple of weeks off from my course-work. My boyfriend is sick, and I'm with him as much time as I can be. He's getting treated here, actually."

"I'm so sorry to hear that," Darl says. "What happened to him? Oh jeez, sorry, that's none of my business."

"No, it's okay. I'll maybe tell you more about it later. But right now, let me see where you are with your studies."

I'm pleased to find Darl's science courses are still quite familiar, even though I'm more than three years out of high school. And helping her with the things she's stuck on proves just the distraction I need.

"You're a great teacher," she tells me after I've spent over an hour covering her lessons in organic chemistry and electrochemistry. "I'm beginning to get some of this stuff."

"That's good. I haven't felt too much like tackling my own coursework lately, so I'm glad I can help you out. How are you doing otherwise?"

Darl hasn't said anything about her medical woes, but she picks up on my cue.

"Oh, this whole thing sucks. They aren't saying too much, but it looks like they aren't going to find a bone marrow match for me. Which means I'm stuck with these transfusions at shorter and shorter intervals. The future looks pretty bleak. I know I could read a whole lot about it on the Internet, but I've made a point of not going there. Burying my head in the sand, you might say, but there you go."

"Seems like an absolutely okay response to me."

"Yeah. My mom's been much the same as me—not reading up on it, I mean. But my dad is downloading everything he can lay his hands on about adults with thalassemia. I know he wants me to talk more about it—it's like he feels I should. But I just tell him I will when I'm ready." She switches the topic back to me. "How come you want to be a doctor?"

I have my answer ready at once. "I'm just a science nerd who wants to care for other people."

"That sounds like a great reason."

Darl and I chat a bit longer, and as I leave her, I think about Jonah's situation, and his family's reactions to it. Once I'd got over the initial shock, I had wanted to know everything I could about his astrocytoma. Especially as it was pretty rare, and it seemed like the treatment was far from set in stone. But I know Ann and Jonah just want to deal with the present situation and leave the rest to the doctors. Ann told me on our drive to the hospital this morning that no amount of reading and quizzing is going to change things. There was for sure no talk about statistics and the like while I was at Jonah's place. After a couple of tries to get Jonah to open up more, I've decided to let it go—at least for now.

For all my reading, it remains a total mystery why this monster has invaded my beloved's body. What the future holds, and whether he is going to be cured and return to normal life is in the hands of his doctors and other caregivers. And God. I've often heard it said God works through doctors—though I'm not sure too many doctors think of it like that. Or if I do. All I can do is love Jonah with all my heart and not try to second-guess what the future holds. That's my kind of praying.

Once Jonah has finished his latest course of chemo, Dr. MacIsaac gives him the okay to head home for another week.

"He told me to stay a million miles away from anyone with a cold, or any other kind of infection," he tells me. "But he thinks I'm safer at home than hanging around here while my blood counts recover. I just have to stay out of restaurants and shopping malls, and make sure you all wash your hands a whole bunch whenever you're around me."

"That's great, Jonah! And it seems like it hasn't been too bad for you this time, right?"

"Yeah, I'm hanging in. Maybe it's true the chemo is easier to handle in your early twenties than it is for those guys we've met on the adult oncology ward. Like Dr. MacIsaac said, I'm still pretty much a kid. If this shit had to happen in our family, far better it picked on me than either Ann or Belinda. And it's get-overable, like I said before."

"I guess so." I hesitate. "Did he say anything about…well, about us still sleeping together?"

"Yeah. I wondered about that too, after he'd made such a big deal about cutting down on close contact and stuff. I went ahead and asked him, and he said it was okay. But that it would be best if we played it cool, and just *slept* together! We didn't get into performance issues." He gives me a wink and we both giggle.

"Well, after our latest experience, maybe we won't find it too hard," I say, squeezing his hand.

I only manage a couple of sessions with my patient buddies before it's time to head off to Port Hawkesbury with Jonah and Ann. But I promise to check back in with them when I get back if they're still in the hospital. Time to talk to my dean, too. He's once again understanding.

"It's close to the end of term now, and you've kept up your high grades. As long as you can complete any outstanding assignments from a distance, you're fine. There's no need for you to be in class. I can even arrange for you to do your final exams online if need be."

I'm delighted to be back with Belinda and Sophie again, to do rounds of the beehives with Ann, and to spend my nights with Jonah. We're happy just holding hands under the covers—pretty much like an old married couple. I'm getting into the habit of sharing household chores with Ann and Belinda and Sophie, though the moms are quick to let Jonah know this is very much a temporary arrangement.

"Don't imagine our Joe gets to be waited on by the women of the household," Belinda tells me. "We're just cutting him some slack while he gets his strength back, right, Joey? We don't want you smashing a whole bunch of dishes."

"Right, Mom. You'll all be able to put your feet up when I'm done with my treatment!"

I ponder the age-old issue of gender roles. Women seem to be taking more and more leadership—at least, in the things that make the world go round. Health and education are all that matter in the end, as far as I can see. And if women are going to be the ones in charge, maybe education and health will finally get the lion-size chunk of the resources.

We return to the city for Jonah's next round of chemo. All in all, he seems to be handling things as well as anyone could hope. He's committed to all the physio exercises he's learned, and I enjoy putting him through his paces. An occupational therapist has started coming by and getting Jonah working on his laptop. She's helping him get back his old dexterity, though texting on his phone quickly exhausts the strength in his left thumb. The chemo courses are more grueling, and Jonah's physical and emotional recovery takes longer each time. Dr. MacIsaac brings up the possibility of missing out the next round altogether, but Jonah won't hear of it.

"I don't want it written on my tombstone 'Here lies a wimp who couldn't hack it.'"

By this time the oncologist is accepting Jonah's particular way of dealing with his situation, with the odd death joke thrown in. "Fair enough," he answers. "We'll just need to spread them out a bit to let your blood counts get back to a safe range. I don't want it to say 'Here lies a hunk and a hero' either. Not that I see tombstones in your future any time soon," he adds quickly.

It's the end of classes and exams are starting when Jonah and Ann next head home, so I stay in Halifax. It's hard to let Jonah out of my sight, but I can't keep him all to myself. His family loves him deeply and needs to spend at least as much time with him as me. Most important, Jonah has his own life to live, his own way forward to discover—or recover.

I've always been a good test taker, unlike some of my friends who get stressed out the week before and during exam week. The deadline is fast approaching for med school applications too. The Canadian schools are even more competitive than in the US where there are so many more to choose from. There are fewer than twenty in Canada and getting into one outside your home province is especially tough. And costs a lot more.

But the dean still seems to think I have a decent chance. He tells me he'll write a strong recommendation letter, given my high grade-point average. A couple of my other professors have agreed to do the same. The two months I spent last summer working at the health food store in Gananoque were great experience, especially when it came to learning about proper nutrition. By the time my summer job was over I was able to give all kinds of advice to customers on healthy eating, and especially what supplements worked and what were an expensive waste of money.

My exam schedule allows me time to catch up with Songlines and with my patient buddies. Several Songlines members live locally, so Raig is committed to having us continue performing through exam week and the holiday season. And it turns out both Timmy and Darl are back in the hospital, Timmy for his two-week course of antibiotics, and Darl for yet more blood. They're also treating her for the overload of iron all these transfusions have caused. I catch up with Timmy first for a couple more mega sessions of video games. I even have his nurse Joanne show me how to do his chest physio to help him get up that gunky mucus.

"There are two main parts to it," Joanne tells me. "The proper terms are postural drainage, percussion, and vibration. But 'tipping and clapping' are what we call it. There's a bunch of different positions to help the mucus drain by gravity from the smaller airways. Timmy knows all this stuff so he'll help if you get stuck."

"I've got it down cold, Ellen," Timmy adds. "No worries."

I can tell he's tickled with the idea of me learning on him, and from him.

"Now I'll teach you to cup your hands so you can bang on each side of his chest," Joanne continues. "See, like this. Timmy knows to let his breath out as slowly as he can."

The nurse raises the end of the bed as he positions himself with the help of several pillows, so his lower body is higher than his chest. Then Joanne places my hands over his left lung and helps me shape them for the cupping movement she has talked about.

"Okay, you're all set. Off you go!"

As I start to clap rhythmically though warily on Timmy's chest, I think about the nurse's ease with such a tricky procedure. How quickly he accepts her instructions, and most of all how willing Joanne is to teach me. I've never thought about the variety of demands that go into a nurse's day. The doctors come and go, maybe a couple of times a day if you're still a resident. But I know the nurses try to be at the bedside at least as much as filling in their endless charts. I think back to that amazing bedside encounter with Beatrix and Dylan. Even if I do get into med school, I'll always be ready to learn from nurses.

Timmy has been getting this treatment at least twice a day every single day of his life, from the time he was diagnosed, even more often when he gets especially congested. And it will continue every day of his life. But even with the most faithful treatment he will be lucky to live far into his thirties. Which would be the worst of these two terrible afflictions—being born with CF, or being diagnosed with cancer as a child? Until a few years ago, before they started finding all the chemo drugs, anyone who got cancer died from it. Most older adults still do. But the cure rate is getting steadily better, while everyone with CF still dies young. Perhaps lung transplants will change that in time, but the treatment for both illnesses can only be thought of as awful. I shake my head to free myself from my morbid thoughts.

I'm especially happy to catch up with my fellow Songlines members on Friday. As soon as the others start telling their stories, I remember why I am deep down glad to be part of this group. I listen as Amy describes her experiences with a ninety-year-old woman, Mrs. Atkins, who is American and had been an avid dancer in her youth. She has leukemia and knows she isn't long for this world. Amy and Dawn have worked up a dance for her, borrowing largely from Martha Graham clips they've found on YouTube, because Mrs. Atkins told them she once saw the world-famous dancer perform.

"We did our best to dance several pieces we found online," Amy tells us. "We both felt shy at first because we were such raw amateurs. But Mrs. Atkins smiled a whole lot and cried some and told us it filled her with joy to watch us. Well, that got us crying too! Even though she knows she doesn't have too much longer, she still takes care with her appearance. She had on a pretty nightie and had done her hair specially. It's wonderful we've been given this chance to spend time with such a beautiful lady."

"Martha Graham had several bouts of bad depression," Dawn adds. "But she said dancing could help anyone who can breathe and has a heart-beat. And how movement never lies."

It's nice to hear Amy opening up. She was looking quite animated as she talked. Then Bill tells us about taking the drums he's made out of gourds into ten-year-old patient Owen's room. "He's pissed off with being here. He kept telling me, 'I hate the hospital, it's a really weird place, I want to get out of here, it's a really weird place…' On and on like that. I told him how I often used my drums to work off negative feelings, and I showed him how much noise you could make on them. After a bit he started banging on one, and he soon got the idea we could be a duo and make crazy music together. He was yelling all the time he was drumming, till one of the nurses showed up to see what was going on. But once she saw what it was all about she just left us to it. She knew Owen was angry about being here, and I guess she thought this would be good therapy for him."

"There's a lot written about drums relieving frustration," I say. "And lifting your mood, giving you confidence. It's great to hear about it working in practice, Bill."

"Absolutely," Dawn says. "And I'm finding playing my autoharp at the bedside's a real comfort to a lot of people. Like it seemed to be for Joe when he was so sick."

"Jonah told me listening to you all sing lifted his spirits a lot," I say. "He's studied a lot about music and healing—how it's maybe the best kind of art for people who are ill. He says there's never been a human culture that didn't make music."

"I'm so happy you could share your music with Jonah," Raig says, looking around at us all. "It's hard to know how to act around a sick friend. Great to just be there with them, quite apart from the music-making."

When I talk about Darl and how down she's become, Raig asks if I want one of the other Songlines members to take over for me. "It's hugely important you look after yourself, Ellen. Important for all of you," she adds, looking around at everyone again.

"No, I'm okay. I'll certainly let you know if it does get too hard. But I'm feeling close to her, and I know she's glad to have me visiting. I like being able to help her with her schoolwork too, when she feels up to it."

The time comes when the last plastic bag of cancer-fighting drugs is hung over Jonah's bed. I've alerted Songlines and a handful of them turn up to cheer him from the doorway. Raig is there with Dawn and Bill, Therese and Vern, and they serenade Jonah with their rendition of "Wintersong," which brings joyful smiles to the faces of onlookers and not a few tears. Music sure can shake the emotions out of hiding.

Nineteen

Four days after the final chemo cocktail has dripped its way into Jonah's veins and hopefully found its way into his brain to kill off any last cancer cells, the fever hits him. Predictably it comes just when Jonah's white blood count is at its lowest and he's at his most vulnerable. A small patch of redness develops around one of his old IV sites on the back of his left hand. I watch it spread over the space of a day to become a dusky swelling more than six inches across. The fever has him dripping with sweat all over his body.

"What's happening is that Jonah has no defences against it," Paula his nurse tells me and Ann out of Jonah's earshot. Not that he's communicating much—he seems to be drifting into some kind of stupor. "Bacteria have found themselves this little home to nest in. And the blood culture just came back positive." She speaks very quietly. "He just might not beat this. You understand?"

"I understand."

Ann stays silent. The resident shows up to check on Jonah. "We may need to move him to the ICU if he has trouble breathing or keeping his blood pressure up. But we have a bunch of antibiotics that should take care of this."

Over the next forty-eight hours there's no sign that these bacteria know they are supposed to crawl off and die. I stay at Jonah's side each night while Ann grabs a few hours' sleep. I watch in horror as a blotchy purple ulcer develops over the site of the swelling in his arm. Several vivid red lines track up toward his armpit. The resident peers at Jonah's arm with his flashlight on his crack-of-dawn visit.

"We should be seeing pus collecting where the infection started out," he tells me. "He just isn't making any—you've got to have normal white cells circulating to make that happen."

Jonah's temperature reaches forty degrees centigrade. He's drifting in and out of consciousness. Ann and I hold vigil on either side of him, take turns moistening his mouth and cooling his face and neck with wet face cloths. Neither of us voices the thought that his last chemo has proved too much for Jonah to handle. That he is losing the battle against the infection that has invaded his whole body. My mind is too numb for tears. I'm aware only of the terror of not even saying a last goodbye to this man I love.

That evening Therese suggests she come by with Vern and Dawn to make some quiet music. Jonah is pretty much out of it, rousing every so often to mumble incoherently but mostly oblivious to his surroundings.

"Dawn can bring her autoharp—she makes wonderfully calming melodies with it."

"That's a great idea," I tell her. "They say even people in coma can hear music. We'll have to get the okay from the staff, though."

I clear it with the staff nurse, and the trio arrives after their classes are done. It's hard to tell if Jonah is aware of his musician friends during their mini concert, but his face definitely grows more peaceful and his breathing slows and steadies. I myself am lulled into a calm place by the sounds of Dawn's autoharp, with Therese and Vern humming in the background. I continue singing quietly to Jonah long after they've left.

After four days of hectic fevers and persistent swelling of his arm, things reach a crisis. Jonah falls into a state of delirium during a turbulent night. He seems to have reached the end of his heroic efforts to keep going. Even the night nurse's soothing words do little to comfort us. Daylight is just lightening the sky beyond the window when Jonah suddenly opens his eyes. "I'm hungry," he whispers.

"Jonah, you're back," I gasp. I hold back from wrapping my arms around him, instead dash out to find Ann, who is napping in the family room. Then I go searching for his nurse. Eva is at the nurses' station giving her report to Paula who is starting her shift.

"He just woke up! He says he's hungry!"

"I'll be right in." Eva is busy checking the computer. She quickly prints off a page of lab reports and hands them to Paula. "And here's his morning blood report. His white count is starting to bounce back!"

Over the next several days Jonah regains much of his old spirits and even his appetite. The swelling in his hand and arm resolves almost as fast as it had appeared, and the ulcer develops a healthy patch of skin over it. Not for the first time I recall what Dr. MacIsaac told us: that kids can handle the hefty chemo doses that would have flattened old guys like him. Even so, it's a miracle—a few little white blood cells reappear in Jonah's blood and he wakes up! But we have to help him with simple tasks like making it to the bathroom. I try not to draw attention to his appearance as I take in how thin and taut the skin over his face and jaw has become, and how much muscle bulk he has lost in his arms and legs.

"I don't remember much about the last few days," he tells me. "But I never want to go through anything like that again. And I'm sure glad to be rid of that tube up my you-know-what."

"They told us they had to catheterize you while you were so sick. It helped make sure your kidneys were working fine and they didn't overload your system with fluids. Paula said this kind of infection can sometimes cause your kidneys to shut down. I tell you, Jonah, I'm learning a lot of hands-on medicine hanging out with you!"

"Better than hitting the textbooks, right? Well, I'd just as soon not have you going to school on me." He stops and reaches out with his good arm to draw me in close. "But when you get through med school, I'll certainly want you for my doctor."

The familiar sensation that signals tears fills my throat and nostrils. It takes three swallows to quell it.

Dr. MacIsaac decides it's safe for Jonah to be out of isolation long enough to repeat the scans that will tell us how far the cancer has shrunk. Could Dr. El Khouri operate again to cut out anything possibly cancerous? We're both at Jonah's bedside that evening when the oncologist comes by to report on the latest MRI findings. He takes his time checking Jonah out to see how well he's healing from his recent crisis and how much strength he's regained in his left side. Then he pulls up a chair and looks at each of us in turn before fixing his gaze on Jonah.

"I'm glad to tell you things look very good, Joe. There's just a small area of abnormal tissue where the cancer used to be. You've responded well to everything we could throw at you." He hesitates a long moment. "But I had a chance to talk with Dr. El Khouri, and he's not in favour of more surgery. I'm sure he'll come and discuss it with you himself, but he thinks going back and trying to dissect out anything left behind would do more harm than good. This cancer has a way of infiltrating your healthy brain tissue. To be sure to leave a clean margin around anything cancerous, he'd have to cut out some healthy parts."

"Alright, but what's going to happen to the stuff you can still see?" Jonah asks at once. "Won't that just grow right back after a bit?"

"There's every possibility it won't, Joe. I'm hopeful any cancer cells left in there are dying off as we speak. Remember what I told you—both the chemo and the radiation go on working even after you're all through with them. No guarantees, mind, I think you know that. But the best possible thing will be for you to head home and work on getting back to a hundred per cent functioning. No reason you couldn't be back in school by next fall."

Jonah makes no comment. He's reluctantly accepted he's not going to graduate in the spring. Dr. El Khouri drops by and tells him pretty much the same as Dr. MacIsaac. Go home and enjoy yourself and get good and healthy again is the clear message.

Belinda is at the wheel when we gather at the hospital entrance, and Jonah climbs with very little help into the front passenger seat. Several Songlines members, together with two of Jonah's nurses and his resident doctor, have joined us to see him off. Belinda gets out and comes round to hug me. A first. She's having a harder time than Ann getting comfortable with me.

"You be sure to come out as soon as your exams are over," she says. "Our boy will be pining for you."

"I'll be there, no worries. Maybe we could have an early holiday celebration? I'm planning to head home to Ontario for Christmas with Mom and Dad."

"That would be fun. Good luck with your exams."

Twenty

It's Belinda who meets my bus as it pulls into the depot late on Friday afternoon. I'd finished my last exam the day before. She hugs me again before taking my bag and dropping it on the back seat. The hug felt a little easier.

"It's lovely to see you again, Ellen," she says as she pulls out of the depot. "I'm on pick-up detail today because Ann and Jonah are busy getting everything ready for the market tomorrow. He's decided baking is better therapy than the computer for getting his strength and agility back. So far he hasn't broken any dishes—and I think he maybe takes after Ann in his culinary skills!"

"He told me on the phone he's been making pretzels, that they'll be a new feature at the market. Have you tried any?"

"You bet. They're delicious! His latest creations are a jalapeno-cheddar mix and some heavily garlic-flavoured ones. You know how those cancer drugs have blunted his taste buds, so he's decided to experiment with stronger flavours."

"I can't wait to be a taste tester," I say, laughing.

As we pull up to the front of the house, Jonah is standing there waiting to greet me. Ann and Sophie hold back to let us have our moment, which proves a long one.

"I've been missing you so, Jonah," I murmur into his ear as I hug him. "And it's only been a week."

"I love you, Ellen. Wow, I love you," he whispers back.

Ann embraces me warmly, then makes way for Sophie who is hovering in the hallway. I reach out spontaneously to hug her too and I feel her respond. This was definitely the right thing to do.

"Okay, what's on the pretzel menu today, Jonah? I've got to give my seal of approval before you try them out at the market."

"Let's see now. We've got a standard toasty twist with a taste of honey and low salt content," Jonah announces as he pulls a covered tray from the pantry. "And for the more adventurous, there's a softer dough variety with a garlic and parmesan filling. Take your pick!"

I waggle my head from side to side, pretending to vacillate. "No way I can decide," I say finally as he pulls out the second tray. "I'll just have to sample one of each." I take a big bite of the more traditional pretzel.

"Jeez, this is good! Crisp on the outside, soft and doughy on the inside. And that salty sweetness." I swallow to make room for another big bite. "You going into business with your mom?"

As I chew, I take a good look at Jonah. He's still skinny as a rail and he has barely a fuzz of hair on his scalp, but I can sense a clear change for the better. He's definitely moving with more freedom. I can hardly recall the nightmare of his battle with the infection that almost did away with him. And finally being free of those grueling months of treatment seems to have lifted a burden. The lines of his face have softened back to their relaxed cheeriness. I've spent more time hunting online for all the latest statistics about his cancer, and I feel sure that right now I'm witnessing the beginnings of Jonah's road to full recovery. None of the family seems at all bothered when I reach over to place another salty-sweet kiss on his lips.

"This is the very best kind of therapy, Jonah," I say as we break apart.

At six-thirty the next morning, we all five crowd into the car and head to the market on the edge of town. It occupies a large horse barn and part of an outdoor arena, which is only used for occasional events. We've filled the trunk with an assortment of freshly baked products and a few jars of honey left over from the fall. We have almost an hour to set things up in Ann's allotted stall, and with five pairs of hands we make short work of it under her direction. We do a lot of jostling and giggling in the confined space around Ann's stall.

"It usually takes me twice as long as this," she says, laughing. "I'm going to bring you guys along to help every time. Though you can take it in turns—having four helpers is overdoing things a tad."

Over the next four hours I meet a dizzying array of people who come by not only to shop but to offer their greetings to Jonah. The news has spread that he's finally through with his arduous treatment. I'm aware that I'm also drawing a lot of attention.

"I hope you're going to open up your practice here in Port Hawkesbury when you get through your training," a local farmer says. "Two of our doctors are talking about retiring, and we'd just love to have some fresh blood around here."

"Well, it could just happen. But first of all, I've got to get accepted into medical school. That's about the biggest hurdle of all."

As we're cleaning up at the end of the morning, Ann says, "Your pretzels were a big hit, Joe. They sold out in the first couple of hours."

"More the novelty factor than anything," Jonah responds, trying to sound modest while clearly delighted to find his newfound skills so appreciated. "I'll see what flavors I can come up with for next week."

Jonah and I both grab a nap that afternoon, but the rest of the day I notice he's taking on small domestic tasks. Even simple things like putting away plates and silverware still take him a while. I watch him lift a plate from the sink and place it with great care on the dish rack.

"That's plastic," I tell him. "It's not going to break."

He grins at me. "Just practicing."

"Great to have you back doing the chores, Joe," Belinda comments from her chair at the table as she enjoys a second cup of coffee on Sunday morning.

"Well, it's good to see you taking it easy, Mom, after a hard week at the office. And it feels great to help out again."

When we're alone, I ask Jonah how his family feels about me showing up so much.

"It's no problem, babe. They're happy to have you here as often as you can make it. It's not just about me and you—they're all falling in love with you. Which doesn't surprise me at all!"

"Well, I'm beginning to feel a real part of your family. But you'll all get a break from me while I'm home for Christmas and New Year."

"Two whole weeks almost. I'll be dying here, babe."

"We'll just have to make this weekend one to remember!"

And so it proves. Jonah's family decides to take up my suggestion of an early Christmas celebration. They find it a welcome diversion to pick out a tree at the market. And their favourite ornaments surface from a box under the stairs. We decorate the house inside and out, including mistletoe and a wreath on the front door. A rich Irish stew simmers on the stove as carols ring out from the radio or CDs. I have to admit the sound quality from their Boss set-up is a whole lot better than my smartphone. The market runs right through until the new year, with hot cider and gingerbread cookies in plentiful supply. Jonah gets back into his baking experiments while I spend more time with Sophie. She's finding it hard to hang out with her friends because they keep quizzing her about Jonah. Some of them have met him and decided he's definitely a babe.

"They even thought his bald head was like some kind of fashion state-ment," she tells me. "As if he didn't have that huge scar right on top!"

We've all decided to find inexpensive fun presents for each other, and Sophie jumps at the chance to go Christmas shopping with me. Over fancy coffees and cookies she starts to open up when I suggest it might be good for both of us to chat some about Jonah.

"I still have a hard time believing it," Sophie says. "And it's so hard to talk about. I mean, I feel bad even bringing things up with you. I know how much you love each other, and I can't imagine what you must be going through."

"Sophie, it does help me to talk about it, especially with someone other than Jonah. Your mom—Ann—and I have been a real support to each other. And the thing is, listening to her, and to you too, helps keep my own thoughts at bay. I think Belinda is coming around too, since she talked to Dr. MacIsaac. Did you hear what she said when she saw the lights on the porch and winding around the cedar trees in front?"

"What?"

"She said how happy she was Jonah would be home for Christmas instead of being stuck in the hospital at the end of a needle, getting horribly sick from chemo."

"Wow, I didn't hear that. Well, I'm glad too. Even though…. Oh, this whole thing sucks."

"*Sucks* pretty much says it. So you and I will have to watch out for each other."

I look at Sophie over her coffee cup. Her eyes are misting. I hand her a napkin in place of the tissues I'm fresh out of.

"It's good chatting together, Sophie. Especially because you're so healthy! I see a lot of teens at the hospital who are terribly ill. Let's be sure to check in with each other a lot, okay?"

"Okay."

After the Saturday market I borrow the family car, and Jonah and I take off to the beach. Jonah thinks he's up to driving—which is quickly nixed by all. There's not a soul around. The water's winter chill, but Jonah decides swimming will be excellent therapy for working his left arm and leg. He has a hard time keeping up with me when I peel off my own clothes and take off in a tumult of splashes to try to get warm. We're like two polar bears come early for the New Year's Day swim. When I splash my way back to see how he's managing, he grabs me in close for a bunch of wet kisses. As we move in tighter for a prolonged hug, I discover Jonah has shivered himself into a very respectable erection.

"Guess you're glad to see me, eh?"

"You bet—and it feels like I'm getting to express my feelings about it."

"Well, we'd better stop in Pharmasave for a good supply on the way home!"

Neither of us can stop laughing until Jonah manages to trip me and I fall backwards underwater with him sprawling on top. We stagger out of the waves, shaking with cold and laughter.

The rest of the family is used to the two of us taking off to bed early, and Jonah can still claim he needs the extra sleep. Not that anyone is asking personal questions about what we get up to once we make our way upstairs. I can tell Jonah is eager to see if he can overcome the major frustration of his last few months. As he climbs in beside me, I feel my own excitement building deep in my belly. We waste little time with preliminaries.

"Hey, babe, maybe it will be easier if I get on top," I whisper as I reach down to lift his penis into my hand. I'm gratified to feel it quickly stiffen.

"Sounds like a plan." Jonah chuckles. "Let you do the work!"

I soon discover this is a very good plan. Once he's inside me I have to work to help keep him hard, and it takes longer for him to come than it had early in our relationship. Which adds a whole lot to my own pleasure. I giggle as we hold each other afterwards.

"I like it that it takes you so long to get there," I whisper. "I'm finding out exactly what all the fuss is about. You be sure to let me know when you're ready to go again!"

We try not to look too blissed out when we come down to breakfast the next morning, but I feel a constant urge to wrap my arms around my lover. I'm proud of the success of our lovemaking, and I'm feeling a buzz of anticipation for the next occasion. After breakfast I call Mom to chat about our Christmas plans.

"Your dad and I are waiting till you're here to go shopping," Mom tells me. "It'll be last minute, but maybe the crowds will be less by then."

"You don't have to make a big deal about things, Mom. I'm just looking forward to seeing you after so long. Are you up for helping with the big Christmas dinner at Crossroads?"

"Wouldn't miss it!" she replies.

I'm pleased to hear we'll be keeping up the family tradition. Thanks to COVID, it's been a couple of years since Crossroads church has been able to host its Christmas charity feast. It is so much in the spirit of the season and will be a lovely way for the three of us to be together. Dad's job as a district social worker has taken him into a lot of the poorer neighborhoods, and I know he will love reconnecting with many families to celebrate.

"I'll get the bus back to Halifax, then catch the early train to Montreal and be in Kingston late afternoon," I tell Mom. "I'll be home before dark on the twenty-third."

As expected, Christmas at home is much quieter than the earlier celebration at Jonah's. Dad is working Christmas Eve, so Mom and I spend much of the day shopping. We want to get the tree decorated and Christmas Eve dinner ready before Dad gets home. This will be our celebration meal and we look forward to working on it together. We deliver a big batch of salad veggies and potatoes to Crossroads, knowing the cooking crew will be starting work at crack of dawn Christmas morning to prepare meals for fifty to a hundred people.

"I'm sorry Dad's not here to help," Mom says as we lay out the food for our family meal on the kitchen counter. "He's missed you a whole lot, you know."

"I know, Mom, but he'll be here in time for Christmas Eve dinner. And I'm happy to spend time with just you. Let's catch up after we've got things going here." I feel a blush rising to my cheeks. "I haven't had time to update you about Jonah. It's going well between us."

"High time we met him. He's through with his treatment, right? And the doctors sound pretty optimistic?"

"Yeah, it's all over. All we can do now is hope and pray and wait-see." I have a vivid flash of the hospital and all Jonah has gone through, with Ann and me mostly helpless bystanders. I bring my thoughts back to the present.

"If he's strong enough, I'm going to bring him to meet you the first long weekend in the new year. He's been after me to make it happen."

Twenty-One

January

After several nights at my parents' home, I make the trip back to Halifax the day before New Year's Eve. Therese and Vern and I celebrate the new year with a couple of bottles of sparkling white wine and movie reruns, but we all hit the sack before midnight. I spend the first week of January working at Pierre's Café on Sackville Street, a few blocks from Ramsay. I had worked there for a short spell last spring, before heading home for the summer, and Pierre, a big boisterous French Canadian from Quebec, greets me with a bear hug on my first day back.

The permanent staff haven't changed, and I quickly get back into the swing of things. I mostly wait tables, though sometimes I'm assigned to washing dishes or even baking pies when one of the staff fails to show. Pierre's is a hangout favoured by students so the tips aren't too generous, but the pace and cheeriness of the place more than make up for it. I work the early shift—seven to three—which means most days I can spend some buddy time in the hospital. Once school is in, I cut back my work hours, but Pierre still welcomes having me come in for the late afternoon and evening shifts on the days I have no scheduled classes.

A good paying job is crucial to afford med school—should any of my applications succeed. My parents have offered to help me financially, but they both take home pretty modest salaries and I'm determined not to accept. I wouldn't be anywhere close to having enough saved for the next four years if it weren't for the money Nana J. left me when she died two years ago. I've tucked it away in a savings account and haven't drawn on it at all for day-to-day expenses.

After my third bus trip to Jonah's home, Ann and Belinda gang up on me and despite my protests insist on paying the bus fare. "Think of it as a contribution to our son's recovery," Ann says. "You're playing a vital part."

Jonah is getting measurably stronger and more agile with his fingers every week, which I can appreciate better now I'm not seeing him every day. He feels fit enough to travel the extra distance and I don't refuse Mom and Dad's offer to pay for the train tickets when we make our promised trip to see them. I'm proud of how normal they make our visit. They are welcoming and solicitous but restrain themselves from quizzing Jonah about his illness. My dad has the whole week off call, and he takes Jonah to his favourite pub for a meal on Saturday night. "You two won't have to fuss with cooking," he tells me and Mom, "and you can catch up with each other." The truth is he wants to get to know Jonah a bit more, figuring he could be looking at his future son-in-law.

In mid-January, Dr. MacIsaac schedules a repeat of Jonah's MRI scan. Ann brings him up and she stays overnight with Therese and me, while Jonah reunites with his own roommates for the night. Two days after the scans, Therese and I are over at the guys' apartment enjoying the breakfast Jonah has prepared when Dr. MacIsaac calls on his cellphone.

"Everything looks good, Joe. No sign of anything new happening. It goes along with how much progress you've made with your rehab. I was impressed when I checked you out."

"D'you think Dr. El Khouri will operate on me again?"

The oncologist is quick to answer. "I talked to him, Joe. He still insists any further surgery on your brain would do more harm than good. But I can't see any reason you couldn't resume your school studies. Maybe start slow and work up to a full course load."

Jonah gets permission to join a couple of classes, even though he's missed the first two weeks of the new term. He moves his things back in with Bill and Vern but spends most nights at my apartment. Therese has no objections, especially when Jonah brings both of us early-morning coffee accompanied by one of his choice pretzels.

The night before my twenty-second birthday Jonah is preparing supper for the three of us and I'm in the bathroom when I hear a choking sound from the kitchen. Then a heavy crash. I rush in to find him on the floor, his head and body twisted stiffly to the right. I stand stunned as his arms and legs and jaw start jerking convulsively, then come out of my shock and move fast. I manage to turn him to his side, make sure his airway is clear and his tongue's not obstructing his breathing. There is blood in his mouth where he must have bitten down on it. I know not to restrain his movements or put anything in his mouth. His pants are soaked with urine.

After several long minutes his spasms cease, and he falls into a deep sleep right there on the floor. Once his colour returns to normal and there's no sign he's choking, I stay on my knees beside him, one fist pressed into my face in an effort not to scream. I become aware of Therese's hands resting on my shoulders. She helps me get his wet pants off and retrieves some dry clothes while I remove his boxers and clean him up. The two of us lift him onto my bed and I cover him with a blanket. I'm murmuring soothing words, probably to calm myself more than Jonah because he hasn't stirred.

"I think maybe it's over," I tell Therese. "But who knows if it'll happen again. Jeez, what is it about birthdays?"

"Are you sure he's been taking his anti-seizure meds regularly?" she asks.

"Yes, I'm sure. I've checked with him a couple of times. And he's been careful not to run out."

Therese leaves me sitting beside Jonah on the bed while she locates the bottle of pills in the bathroom. "Are these they?" she asks.

"Yes. Dilantin. It looks like there aren't too many doses left, though, and his doctor at home probably hasn't called in refills to a pharmacy here. Anyway, I think we should have him seen at the hospital once he comes around. They'll want to know what's happened, and maybe change his prescription or up the dose."

"I'll ask Vern to drive us over to Emerg," Therese says. "I don't think we need to call an ambulance, do we?"

"No, it looks like the immediate danger's over. It would be great if Vern could take us though. I'll let Jonah's mom know what's happened."

Thirty minutes later Jonah is stretched out on a gurney in the hospital emergency room, still peacefully asleep. He has straps fastened around his chest and legs in case of a further seizure. A nurse has checked out his vital signs and reassured us everything looks stable. I've talked to Ann and promised to phone her back just as soon as Jonah's been seen. When the on-call doctor appears, I explain who we are and take the lead in describing what's happened. But Therese has to come to my rescue more than once when I become too upset to talk.

"When did you say Dr. MacIsaac last saw him?" the resident asks me as he finishes examining Jonah. I sense he's trying to go slow questioning me, but that this isn't his usual ER modus operandi. He is tall and skinny and everything he does seems to be at double-time.

"I'm sorry, I'm not thinking too straight. Let's see, it was less than a month ago. He had just had follow-up scans and Dr. MacIsaac told Jonah they all looked great."

"Okay. Well, it might just be that Joe needs a stronger seizure medicine, and we can certainly take care of that. But we'll need an EEG to look at the electrical activity in his brain."

"He had a couple of those when all this first happened."

I hold back from telling him that I've had several classes in neurophysiology and know all about EEGs.

"Right. When did Dr. MacIsaac plan to see him next?"

"He told Jonah he'd be seeing him every two months for a good while. His next appointment is in March."

"When I've got the EEG all set, I'll put in a call to his resident to let her know what's happened. See if Dr. MacIsaac wants to see him sooner."

Jonah is starting to stir, blinking his eyes and rolling them back and forth. The doctor lays a hand on his shoulder and brings his face down close.

"Hey, buddy," he says quietly. "You're in the hospital. You had another seizure, but you're okay. We're taking care of things."

"Head hurts," Jonah mutters. He goes to sit up but the restraints around his body stop him short. "What…"

"We had to make sure you didn't fall off or do anything to injure yourself. We can undo these straps pretty soon."

Two hours later he's fully alert, though still complaining of headache. He makes a trip to the bathroom with our help and throws up the almost nonexistent contents of his stomach. The nurse gets him settled again, and after almost an hour the ER doc reappears to check on him.

"Who will be with him if I let him go home?"

"I won't be leaving his side."

He hands me the new anti-seizure prescription. "Okay. But I want to get the first dose of this new medication into him before he leaves. I'll have you hang out in the waiting area for half an hour to make sure it stays down and that everything else is stable."

Vern heads to the hospital pharmacy to get the new script filled while Therese and I help Jonah settle in a seat in the waiting room.

"I just remember starting to prepare supper. Then I felt weird, almost like some kind of out-of-body experience. Next thing I knew I was waking up in here." He makes a clumsy effort to hug me. "Thanks, guys. Thanks for looking after me—and keeping me a million miles away from my truck!"

"Maybe they'll let you drive it again someday," I say. "But it won't be for a good long while. You might want to find out what you can get for it."

"My mom's been after me to sell it too, but I'm pretty attached to those wheels."

"It was probably just that the Dilantin stopped working. You need the stronger medicine, like the doc said."

"I guess so."

Two days later, Dr. MacIsaac's resident phones Jonah to tell him what Dr. MacIsaac said about the EEG.

"It shows a whole lot of electrical activity in the area where you had your original tumour," she tells him. "But Dr. MacIsaac thinks it's no more than you'd expect after your surgery and everything. He does want to move up your appointment, though, and he's going to arrange for another MRI scan in the meantime. Just to be sure there's nothing new going on. Okay?"

Ann comes up to stay again before the appointment, and she and I go with Jonah for the new Xrays, then to Dr. MacIsaac's clinic three days later. Even though the clinic looks full, the doctor doesn't keep us waiting. But just as he's ushering the three of us back to an exam room, a colleague of his slips in with his own patient. The rest of the exam rooms are full, so we have to stand in the passageway making idle chat for several minutes.

Dr. MacIsaac is clearly not going to talk about Jonah's current situation till we're settled in the room, but something in his manner sends a shaft of fear through me. I grip Jonah's right hand as he leans against the wall between me and Ann.

Once a room comes vacant and Jonah is up on the exam table, Dr. MacIsaac asks him about the latest happenings. Jonah updates him on how he's been doing. I have to help him with the details because he's quite confused about the past week. The oncologist puts Jonah through a much more thorough physical than on the last couple of visits.

"I'm not sure I'm quite as strong on my left side, Doc," Jonah says. He hasn't mentioned this to me or Ann. "And I've had a few more headaches lately. Mornings mostly, but they don't last too long."

"Yeah, I agree with you, Joe. Your left side is a bit weaker than when I last saw you. Though that could just be the effect of this latest seizure."

Once he has finished his exam, Dr. MacIsaac glances over at me and Ann. We're perched on chairs behind him near the door. Then he sits back on his swivel stool and turns his full attention to Jonah.

"Joe, there does seem to be something new going on with your latest scans. I've gone over it very carefully with both Dr. El Khouri and the radiologist." He stops talking for a long moment. "Look, we think the cancer might be growing again. It's not definite, but we need to follow things very closely over the next month or two."

I can't stop myself. "What do you mean, not definite? How could it not be definite one way or the other?"

Dr. MacIsaac swings his body back towards me. "I'm sorry, Ellen, it's just that sometimes it can be that way. Medicine isn't the exact science we would all like it to be. And that's even true for MRIs. Like I said, though, about the increasing weakness in Joe's arm and leg—well, the same could be true of these X-ray findings. It could be simply a leftover from Joe's recent seizure. The only way we can be absolutely sure is to wait and see."

"What will you do if it has come back?" Jonah voices all our thoughts. He has managed to pull himself up to a sitting position.

Dr. MacIsaac swivels back to face him. "I think we should talk about that only if and when it proves to be the case."

"Doc, I need to know. We all do. I mean about what other things you've got tucked away in your toolbox. We need to prepare ourselves in case… well, just in case." His voice trails off and he looks expectantly at the doctor.

"You know, Joe, most people in your situation would rather go along with the wait-see plan." Dr. MacIsaac slides his stool up closer and fixes his gaze on Jonah. "But you want the straight scoop. Perhaps your mom and Ellen do too. Okay, I'll be fair and square with you. When it comes to cancer treatment, we always use the very best we have up front. We can't give you any more radiation, not after the doses you've already received from Dr. Davis. And Dr. El Khouri is quite clear further surgery is out for right now. "It all comes down to different drug therapies. We have a couple of new ones tucked in our toolbox, as you call it. But I'd be lying to you if I said they could cure you if the cancer has returned."

"You mean…that would be it. It would just a matter of time." Jonah is holding the doctor's gaze.

"Yes, Joe. Yes, that is what I mean."

I stare down at the floor, my heart pounding, unable to look directly at Jonah lest I catch his gaze.

Twenty-Two
February

After Dr. MacIsaac's gone, Ann and I climb up on each side of Jonah's exam table. We hold him in a long silent clasp. He sits quietly between us, breathing deeply and slowly. Ann isn't holding back tears. How long will it be before a nurse appears saying she needs the room? Perhaps Dr. MacIsaac has told them not to disturb us. Can we stay like this, in this safe place? Can we just stop time?

At last I grab a bunch of tissues from the box on the bed table, take a couple of forceful snorts, and look directly at Jonah and Ann. Ann follows my lead, grabs her own wad, and wipes her nose and the rest of her face. She breaks the silence.

"He's a straight shooter, that Dr. MacIsaac. And you were right, Joe, to make sure he gave us the full scoop. What we should do right now is head home and get our thinking caps on straight."

"Sounds good," Jonah says, his voice shaky but clear. "There's nothing certain right now, like he said. Wait-see is the name of the game. Why don't you give Belinda a buzz at her office, Mom, and let her know what's happening?"

After Jonah has set the date with the receptionist for his three-week appointment, we head for the multi-storey hospital parking lot. None of us can remember what level we left the car on.

"Let's just take the elevator to the top," Jonah says. "Then we can walk down checking each bay."

Playing this hide-and-seek kind of game proves a good distraction, and the other two cheer when I spot Ann's car sitting in the far corner on the third floor.

"Ah, of course, now I remember exactly." Ann laughs. "I guess we're all pretty scattered right now."

"Probably happens to a lot of people around here," Jonah says.

We stop off at both Jonah's and my apartments to pick up clothing and other essentials. I stick a note for Therese on the front of the fridge. Jonah texts Vern and Bill to tell them he's heading home and will fill them in later. He labours over it but won't let me take over. I'm not up to going by the dean's office to explain that I'm once more dropping out of in-person classes. Easy enough to call in from Jonah's place tomorrow. Ann hasn't taken the time to phone Belinda, so Jonah calls her office once we're on the road. She's in a meeting with her boss but phones back thirty minutes later.

"Look, there's nothing definite to report, Mom," Jonah tells her. "It's just there's some weird stuff on the new scans and Dr. MacIsaac says he wants to watch it closely."

Both Ann and I know Jonah is soft-pedalling it. Belinda would more than likely lose it right there in her office if he spelled out what we strongly suspect. Dr. MacIsaac's attempt at reassurance has not put any of our minds at rest.

We gather around the kitchen table before supper that evening so we can all talk. Sophie is soon in tears. Ann wraps her arms around her without attempting to check her sobs. Belinda comes around to where Jonah and I are sitting close together, squeezes in between us to hug us both. One thing about this awful situation—it's put an end to any barriers between Belinda and me.

Jonah starts the conversation. "Okay, the doc was completely honest with us once I told him I wanted to hear it straight up. He gave us the worst possible scenario, sure, but he also told us there was nothing certain. Wait-see is the deal right now. Meantime, I don't want a lot of long faces around here till I head back up to Halifax next month." He summons his lopsided grin and eyes each of us. "Don't go quizzing me morning, noon, and night about how I'm feeling, okay? I'll be sure to let you know if there's anything new to report. Right now, I seem to have worked up an appetite—I haven't had a decent meal since I was last home. Hey, don't take that too personally, babe," he adds quickly when I give him a playful punch on the shoulder.

We all do our best to go along with Jonah's wishes. Even when we cuddle up together in bed, I resist checking how hard it is for him to change positions or tug on the bedclothes when they've shifted over to my side. I'm thrilled he needs only a little help climbing on top our first night back home.

"Oh, Jonah, Jonah, Jonah, I love you," I murmur as his body moves rhythmically above me, and my own starts to respond. Then, "Oh my, oh my, oh my," as he finally slips from me and we lie close side by side. "One way to find out how well your body is working!"

Which sends us into near guffaws until I shush us, embarrassed our noises of pleasure and hilarity will carry to the rest of the house.

There is heavy snowfall in early February, and Jonah and Sophie and I take to snowshoeing in the nearby woods and farmlands. Jonah's left side is still weak, but the ski poles help him balance and Sophie and I don't have to slow down too much. His biggest problem is still with small hand movements, which isn't a big problem for grasping a ski pole. We pull two sleds out of the woodshed, don parkas, toques, scarves, and gloves, and take off sledding in the moonlight. We choose a gentle slope and I share a sled with Jonah, perching behind him to make sure he doesn't tumble, while Sophie leads the way on the other one. It's a perfectly clear night and the snow glistens about us in the moonlight. Our downward glissade only ends when our sled turns turtle and Jonah and I topple into a giggling heap. Sophie glides to a graceful halt at the bottom of the slope. Sophie and I haul the sleds back up while Jonah takes his time clambering slowly behind us.

There are many animal tracks along the woodland trails, and I discover both Jonah and Sophie are experts. They can recognize a fox from a dog and even a coyote. Sophie points out a raccoon print to me, which resembles a very small human handprint. The deer tracks are mostly easy to tell because of their size, but they are often distorted.

"It's because they put their hind feet right down on top of the front ones," Sophie tells me. Sometimes we spot small heaps of their scat nearby. I think it's rabbits till Sophie puts me right.

"Where did you learn all this?"

"Girl Guides mostly. I've been on a couple of overnight camps, even in the winter." She's obviously pleased to show off her expertise. "But I never know whether to be glad or sorry when we don't find any bear tracks."

We make it to the beach in our winter gear a couple of times, though none of us has any interest in stripping off into swimsuits and joining the polar bear club. We make several dozen snow angels, and Jonah creates what he calls a moose angel by keeping one leg clear. Neither Sophie nor I can figure what's especially moose-like about it. On Valentine's Day Jonah gives me a red fleece-lined hoodie-cum-blanket that covers my whole body. There's almost room for him to get inside with me. Ann prepares a dinner of cheese and spinach spaghetti pie, followed by heart-shaped frosted cupcakes. We're blessed with several cold sunny days over the rest of February. Jonah and I spend time walking on Riley's or Port Shoreham beach and wandering through the forest preserve near the back of the house, enjoying the wintry beauty of the bare trees. Great exercise for us both. There are ice patches around the base of many of the trees, and it's easy to see roots that are mostly covered by shrubs in the summer. Other members of the family sometimes tag along, but by unspoken agreement they mostly leave the two of us to ourselves.

The winter foliage is a blend of soft greys and greens and browns. Having been raised in this rural part of the province, Jonah's delighted he can identify the different kinds of maples and birches scattered among the junipers and cedars. We watch a deer emerge from behind a group of evergreens, regard us without fear, then twist its elegant head and disappear once more. We kneel to sift through last year's leaf fall to locate fragile skeletal specimens for Ann's collection of pressed botanicals. Several are whittled down to their veins.

"How long will these last if we just leave them lying here?" Jonah wonders.

"Why don't we do just that?" I answer. "We'll come back and look for them again next year."

"I like that. We'll let them lie in wait for us."

He leans in to kiss me. The kiss lingers until the rattling caw of a crow in the tree right above us breaks the moment.

When Jonah takes naps in the afternoon I put in time on my online courses. It's still crucial to keep up my grades through my final year, even though the die may well be cast as far as scoring one of those precious spots in med school. When I took the MCAT in January my score was under five hundred—not too competitive, but I console myself that I can retake it in April. I'm resolved to be better prepared next time around.

Ann and I accompany Jonah for his appointment with Dr. MacIsaac. Jonah hasn't complained of anything new, and the doctor gives him a good report.

"But I want to get another MRI right before I see you next time, Joe. I'll have my resident set it up, and she'll phone you with the time you need to check in to X-ray."

The weekly farmers' market stays open through the winter months, and Jonah keeps busy creating his fancy pretzels while I help Ann with other baking tasks. I relish the easy kitchen conversation and companionship between the three of us.

"This is a great diversion," Jonah says. "Keeps my mind off too much thinking."

I'm struggling to do the same. We keep the chat well away from any future what ifs.

Twenty-Three

March

A week after his last appointment Jonah wakes in the morning with a blinding headache. I hurry into the bathroom for a moist facecloth to try to ease it, only to find him right behind me.

"I've got to throw up. Quick."

He crouches over the toilet bowl and starts retching. I get down beside him, wrap the wet cloth over the back of his neck, stroke his back rhythmically the way I've watched nurses comfort their patients. Jonah goes on gagging and spitting up his stomach contents till the urgency seems to pass.

"Where's it hurt worst, Jonah?"

"Dunno. All over. It's easing a bit, but it felt like my head was going to split open when I woke up."

"What have you got for pain around here? Anything left from those pills they gave you when you first came home from the hospital?"

"Could be. Can you hunt around a bit?"

"Of course. How about you try lying down again?"

I help him settle back in bed and lay a freshly moistened facecloth over his forehead. Next to his anticonvulsant meds I find a bottle of naproxen with two or three pills at the bottom. The expiry date is two months ago. I go back into the bedroom. Jonah's eyes are closed and he's breathing steadily.

"These would probably be okay, Jonah," I tell him, "though they're a bit out of date. Can you hang on while I check with your mom?" I know Belinda will have already left for work and dropped Sophie at school, but I can hear Ann puttering in the kitchen.

"Yeah. I'm okay right now. You go ahead. Thanks, babe."

I tell Ann what's been happening. She at once reaches into the cupboard above the fridge. It's full of medical and first aid supplies of every kind. She reaches down a bottle from the front and takes out two.

"Motrin, 400 milligrams. Will that do the trick?"

"Ibuprofen, yes. He can certainly take two. Remember they gave them to him in the hospital when they were tapering him off the opioids—they worked well. They should do fine as long as he can keep them down." I catch Ann's scared look and reach in to hug her. I feel a sheen of sweat break out around my own neck and forehead. "Maybe you want to come up with me?" I murmur as I release her.

Jonah sleeps through a good part of the morning. I prop myself up on three pillows with my laptop open on my knees and try to concentrate on my biostatistics coursework. Three weeks to go before the start of finals. Jonah wakes and heads for the bathroom. He stumbles in the doorway like he's about to topple over. I slam my laptop aside and leap off the bed.

"Hang on, Jonah. Let me give you a hand, okay?"

I help him the rest of the way to the toilet, then go back into the bed-room, leaving the door ajar so I can hear him at once if he needs help.

"You doing okay in there?" I call after a few minutes.

"Yeah, I'm making it," he answers after a long pause. His voice is slurring. "My head's bothering me again, though. And my eyesight is a bit blurred. Can you get me a couple more of those pills?"

"I've got them right here. You can take two of these extra strength Motrin three or four times in twenty-four hours."

Jonah stays in bed the rest of the day and sleeps restlessly through the night. By next morning his headache has settled to a dull throb. He is able to keep another dose of the pain meds down but he's too nauseous to swallow anything more than water. Ann and I help him get propped up in bed with a bunch of pillows. It makes his headache less intense than when he lies flat.

"I contacted Dr. Goldmann's office, but she's got no free appointments today," Ann tells Jonah. "She suggests we go to our local Emerg so they can check you out. They can maybe write you a prescription for something stronger."

"That'd be good, Mom. Thanks."

I'm relieved Jonah hasn't raised any objections to Ann's suggestion. "I think we should also call Dr. MacIsaac's office," I say.

"Let's see what they say in Emerg first."

"That'd be good," Jonah repeats. He isn't processing things very fast. His voice is definitely slower and less clear. Could be the drugs, but I keep this thought to myself.

The emergency room is mercifully quiet this early in the morning, and the on-call doctor keeps us waiting less than fifteen minutes. A tall guy of maybe forty with a free and easy manner, he's dressed in jeans and a dark blue shirt with no tie or white coat.

"I'm Barry Cameron. Sounds like you're having a hard time, Joe. I went ahead and pulled your records, so I'm pretty up to date with your story. But go ahead and tell me what's been happening lately."

Jonah goes over the last twenty-four hours. I fill in the details when he gets confused or can't get his words out easily. I have to prompt him to tell the doc about his blurring vision, and Jonah doesn't correct me. Dr. Cameron quizzes him about exactly when and where the headache is worst, and anything else that seems new. He spends several minutes peering into the back of Jonah's eyes with his ophthalmoscope.

"I'm sorry, Joe, I know this light is hard to put up with," he says when Jonah starts tearing up.

"You got that right."

"I'm almost done, okay?"

As soon as he's finished his exam the doctor pulls his chair up close to Jonah. He stays silent a long moment. I have a chilling image of Dr. MacIsaac going through the same motions at our last visit.

"Look, Joe," Dr. Cameron says finally, "There's some abnormal swelling at the back of your eyes. We call it papilledema. That's why your vision's been a bit blurred. And it explains your headaches." He glances over at Ann and me. "I have to tell you, it's not a good sign. It almost certainly means there's pressure building up in your brain."

I reach to grasp Ann's hand, feel her responsive squeeze. I continue to hang onto it.

"We need to get you up to the university hospital right away," the doctor continues. "But first I'm going to get an IV started and give you a big dose of Decadron. That's a corticosteroid and it will reduce the swelling fast."

Jonah has closed his eyes against the overhead light, but they're still tearing. He wipes at them with the bundle of tissues I hand him.

"They gave him that after his brain surgery," I tell Dr. Cameron. "To cut down the swelling, like you said."

"Right. So let's get things started, then I'll call Dr. MacIsaac's office to let him know—"

Jonah interrupts him. "It's back, isn't it? The cancer."

"Joe, I can't say that for certain. Only the experts can. But you'll certainly need more scans right off. And yes, I'm sorry to say it is very possible."

Ann finds her voice. "I guess we can't take Joe in the car, not with an IV running, right?"

"No, we need to get an ambulance for him. But one of you can go with Joe and the other one behind in your car. They'll be travelling pretty quick, okay, so don't go breaking any speed limits yourself."

Once the two paramedics in charge of the ambulance have Jonah strapped onto a gurney and have hung his IV, I sit in the back beside him. My seat is facing away from the direction we're going, and I have my own seatbelt fastened tight. The paramedic in the passenger seat tells us he will hear me right away if I need him. Fifteen minutes into the ride Jonah tells me his headache is easing up, so the steroids must be kicking in. He sleeps the rest of the way while I hold his free hand, well aware of the hectic speed we are going. A little over two hours after we'd set out, we are back in the university hospital ER. The triage nurse, Gina, greets us as soon as the paramedics wheel Jonah into the waiting area.

"We've been expecting you, Joe. Dr. Cameron called ahead to say you were on your way. I'm sorry to hear you're having trouble." Then to the paramedics, "You can go ahead and wheel him back to room four."

Dr. MacIsaac's resident shows up just as the ER doctor is starting to check Jonah out. "I know Joe well, Carl," she tells her colleague. "I'll be happy to take over."

"Thanks, Renalda, that'd be good. I've got a full slate of other customers right now."

"I agree with Dr. Cameron," Renalda tells Jonah after she's finished her own exam. "Your optic discs are definitely a bit swollen. Papilledema, like he told you. I've talked to Radiology, told them we need an MRI as soon as possible. Meanwhile we'll keep you resting here. You need anything more for pain right now? Not wanting to throw up?"

"Guess not right now," Jonah says. "It's eased up a good bit." Neither he nor I mention we know what papilledema implies.

"Okay, I know you've got a whole ton of questions," Renalda says. "But it'd be best if we wait till after they've run the scans. Then Dr. MacIsaac will answer everything you want to know. Everything. Okay?"

Jonah and I know she's right. She can't tell us anything new that we aren't already pretty clear about, so we hold back on quizzing her. As soon as she's taken off, Jonah opens an eye and looks at me.

"How d'you reckon they spell that word?"

I catch the impish grin on his face: he's looking to lighten things up. Our growing dread could quickly turn to panic if we let it. I find it in myself to go along with his attempt at silliness.

"Er…well, let's see, um, p…p…u…u…l…l…l…i…p… No, I give up. Why don't you tell me."

"Hey, you're the hotshot doc-to-be. I'm just the little ole patient here."

"Hotshot doc-to-be *maybe*. Big maybe."

"Babe, you're gonna make it. I know about these things."

He closes his eyes and I sit holding his free hand. Then I close my own and focus on my breathing, not letting my thoughts run on to… to what?

"You wanna get it on, babe?" Jonah says suddenly. His eyes are still closed. "There's plenty of room on this gurney."

I open my own eyes. Jonah's grin is back.

"Sure. It'll have to be a quickie, though. I don't think they'll let me in the MRI machine with you. Could wreck the pictures."

"Might make some pretty nice ones—kinda soft porn. Probably fetch a good price."

We both snort, trying to stifle the noise.

"Sometimes you just gotta laugh, right?" Jonah says as we sober up.

I bring my lips down to his and kiss him for some time. There's a lot of entangling of tongues.

"Just you wait till I get you home, feller."

We're interrupted by the curtain being drawn back. But it's not the nurse, it's Ann. She's taken forty-five minutes longer to get here than the runaway ambulance.

"No speeding, I hope, Mom?" Jonah quizzes her.

"Drove just barely over the speed limit the whole way. Boy, you guys sure took off, though. Okay, what's the scoop?"

"Same old, same old. MRI time, folks!"

I shift over so Ann can move in and hug Jonah. "How're you feeling, hon?"

"Headache's better. Has to be those wonder steroids. I'm keeping water down too, so that's good."

The curtains flip back again. It's Gina with one of the nursing assistants.

"They're ready for you, Joe."

Jonah and his gurney disappear into the elevator restricted to staff and patients while we take the stairs to Radiology in the basement. We try not to listen in on the conversation between the two doctors ahead of us. They look like residents, and we can't help overhearing "the gallbladder in forty-four" and "my GI bleed in fifteen."

Doesn't anyone teach them not to gossip about their patients around visitors? I hope I never catch myself doing that. At least they aren't identifying them by name.

Everything in the X-ray department is taking on a depressingly familiar look. Jonah has made altogether too many trips down here. And now they will probably put him back up in ICU just in case things go sideways. I don't finish the thought about exactly what sideways might look like.

Dr. MacIsaac shows up early in the evening with Renalda. He spots us in our usual spots outside the ICU door as soon as he exits the elevator.

He ushers us in ahead of him to Jonah's room. The MRI exam has gone smoothly, and a new ICU resident has already gone over Jonah's whole story from start to finish. Then the ICU attending had gone through it with the resident and carried out what would be Jonah's fourth physical of the day. Everyone seems to come up with the same findings and give Jonah the same story: wait on the MRI report, Dr MacIsaac will be coming by shortly, meanwhile keep the IV Decadron and fluids running, pain meds, anti-nausea meds, anti-seizure meds, you name it.

Dr. MacIsaac keeps his own exam blessedly brief, then perches close by Jonah's bed. Renalda stands behind him, and Ann and I right opposite on the other side.

"I guess you've been put through the wringer today, Joe. I don't need to repeat everything. Did anyone else talk to you about your scan?"

"Nope. Looks like the buck stops with you."

"Right." He goes through his familiar ritual of quietly eying Jonah, then glancing at Ann and me. "I've got bad news, Joe. I'm sorry," he says without preamble. "Your cancer is back."

He says no more, simply keeps his gaze on Jonah. I reach to grasp Ann's hand. Some merciless, death-dealing force is set to explode inside—inside my belly, my chest, my throat, my skull. The feeling expands, threatens to crush the life from me. As I pull in a deep breath to fight it off, the hideous experience starts as suddenly to dwindle and die. I'm in total emptiness. Barely aware of the room, of Ann returning my clasp, of the enduring silence between the doctor and his patient. My beloved, whom I want to never, ever lose. With whom, if it is to be, I want to enter eternity.

Joe is the first to break the deep hush. "I guess we've figured out how to spell *papilledema*, Ellen and me."

Oh, you dear goofy guy, you're still finding it in you to make jokes.

I have the strongest impulse to leap up and grab him in my arms. I hold back. The dialogue between Jonah and his doctor is barely begun. Time enough to hold him. To never let him go. Ann and I—mother and lover—are almost intruders. At the very least helpless bystanders.

Dr. MacIsaac blinks once, gazes at Jonah a further long moment, then starts talking again. He's come up with his own response to Jonah's goofiness. "You're a better man than me then, Joe. Spelling is definitely not my strong suit."

The tension and sense of unreality in the room lessen. I grab a handful of tissues from the box on Jonah's bed table, hold them to my eyes, then to my nose, and honk. I feel momentary relief at expelling snot, tears, and emotion all at once. I pass the box to Ann who holds her own wad briefly up to her face, then reaches over to lay a hand on her son's arm. It's question time.

"What exactly does the MRI show?" I ask Dr. MacIsaac.

He turns slightly in his seat to look at me, gathers his thoughts.

"We can see new tumour growing in the original site. In Joe's forebrain, on the right side, where it started out. Right under where Dr. El Khouri operated. But it's also spreading backwards and down deeper into his brain. It's still small though—maybe a couple of centimetres max."

Jonah speaks again, but this time there's no goofiness. "I want to see it, Doc. My scans, I mean."

"Of course. Absolutely," Dr. MacIsaac turns to his resident. "Renalda, can you head down and bring up some of the clearer images so we can go over them together?"

As she takes off, Ann shifts her chair back so I can move in closer to Jonah. Jonah lifts his right arm and wraps it around me. I continue putting the questions the others aren't ready to pose.

"What's next, Dr. MacIsaac? Once we've had a chance to see Joe's pictures. I mean, what treatment are you planning?"

"Ellen, that's something Joe and I need to go over very thoroughly. He needs a chance to think about all the possible things that could happen —good and not so good. There are a few options for Joe and all of you to think about. But the very first thing is for the three of you to try to get some rest. Nothing more's going to happen tonight. Let's sit down again first thing in the morning. I'll lay it all out, all the treatment possibilities. Then Joe will be fully prepared to make decisions."

Renalda reappears carrying several X-rays. Dr. MacIsaac holds each of them up to the overhead light.

"Can you see them all right, Joe?"

Jonah peers at the pictures. The images of his own brain. Ann and I lean in closer so we can get a better look.

"It's hard to see things clearly without a lit-up screen in front of us," Dr. MacIsaac says. "But I think you can get a pretty good idea. We can go down and look at them in Radiology tomorrow if that's what you still want to do."

The oncologist starts to outline the normal brain tissue within the black oval casing of Jonah's skull. We all gaze at the labyrinthine outlines of grey, white, and dark material that some unimaginably complex computer has generated. I breathe deep to counter gathering nausea at these terrifying images of my loved one's brain. Images that are bringing terrible truths to the light of day.

Is this the right thing to be doing? Or has Jonah gone literally out of his mind—demanding right off to see in black and white this monster that is threatening to snatch him away from me? I compel myself to stare at the lifeless images—the very core of Jonah's thinking and feeling self. As Dr.

MacIsaac outlines the normal parts, I steel myself for what he's about to highlight. Jonah is holding me close against his side but seems totally rapt by what the doctor is demonstrating.

"Now, you see up here in the front, Joe, where Dr. El Khouri took a small flap of your skull away when he operated. Underneath that, that white stuff with the mostly irregular edges—that's the cancer. It should all look grey, like most of your brain tissue does. You see how it stretches backwards a bit, then kind of peters out as it merges with all your normal brain substance."

He stops talking as Jonah takes one of the X-ray films from him and studies it silently, moving it about a little to catch the light. He hands it back, leans against his pillows, looks at each of us in turn before bringing his attention back to Dr. MacIsaac.

"Thanks, Doc. I needed to see what this thing looks like. But I guess I've seen enough. You're dead right, we've got a lot of talking to do, the three of us. Before you come back tomorrow with the scoop about what we do next."

Dr. MacIsaac shifts his chair back and musters a grin. "I don't get to do this too often, Joe. Give my patient an anatomy lesson on their own brain. Let alone their brain cancer. I guess you don't want to duck things, do you?" He glances again at Ann and me, seems about to address us, thinks better of it as he takes in the tense looks on our faces. "Enough for tonight. I'll be back first thing. See if you can all get some sleep."

After he and Renalda head out, Ann gets up to switch off the harsh overhead light, leaving only the subdued lighting each side of Jonah's bed. The three of us sit quietly holding each other's hands.

"Jonah, the doctor's right, there's nothing we need to decide tonight. But whatever you end up doing, it will be you calling the shots. You and

Ellen. Belinda and I and Sophie will go along with whatever you decide to do next."

"Thanks, Mom. And thanks for letting me get a close-up view of this thing without you falling apart."

I fasten my arm even tighter around Jonah. "Your mom's right, babe, whatever's going to happen, you'll be in charge. I'm not going to try to tell you what to do." I stop talking, swallow several times to tamp down the sobs rising out of my chest. "But I'm right here with you. You and me, babe."

Twenty-Four

The three of us talk quietly as the dusk closing in beyond the window reminds us another day is ending. Another day of how many ahead? No way to know. I haven't begun to come to terms with this latest bombshell. Ann stays silent. Jonah shifts his body about on top of the bedclothes, still finding it in himself to summon up moments of optimism, even levity.

"Well, that Decadron is holding up well. No headaches right now, no throwing up, no funny vision. Maybe that's all it takes—a dose of Decadron a day keeps the doctor away! And this fluid they've got running into me is making me pee up a storm, so at least they don't have to stick a catheter back in my bladder. In fact, I need to make another pit stop. Don't want to pee the bed."

"Need help getting there?" his mother asks him.

"No worries, Mom. Ellen's had plenty of practice at it." He edges his legs onto the floor as I unplug the IV tubing and wheel the stand behind him. Once I'm sure he's not going to topple over, I pull the bathroom door shut behind him. Ann looks at me.

"You think you can get some shut-eye?"

"I need to try. I'm too tired to think straight."

"They'll be shooing us out of here very soon. And none of us has eaten anything all day. We should probably get a bite."

Jonah overhears his mother as he emerges from the bathroom. "That'd be good, Mom. I'm going to try and crash too. Or I'll maybe watch something on Netflix if the Wi-Fi signal's strong enough. We're not going to settle anything tonight, not till Doc MacIsaac gives us the full scoop. Why don't you guys take off for supper?"

"What do you think, Ellen? Are you up for it?" Ann asks.

"I guess so. I should try and eat something before I get my head down."

I turn into Jonah for a goodnight kiss, keeping it short in Ann's presence.

We try a pub I've never been to, where I'm pretty sure I won't run into anyone I know. I'm not up for telling anyone else the story, let alone dealing with words of sympathy, no matter how well-intentioned. We manage most of a Greek salad and an order of French fries between us, washed down with two seven ounce glasses of white wine. I text Therese to tell her we'll be at the apartment at least for tonight and I'll fill her in on the details. Ann phones home from the apartment and talks to Belinda. It takes several minutes to get Belinda calm enough to hear what Ann is telling her.

"We just don't know anything yet, love. Only that yes, the cancer's back, but it's still very small. We're going to try to get some sleep, then first thing in the morning Dr. MacIsaac will lay out the options for more treatment."

From the bedroom I can hear Belinda's anxiety on the other end of the phone. Ann continues to talk quietly.

"I'll fill you in tomorrow just as soon as we know more. Talk to Sophie a bit about it. She has the right to know and it'll help you to share it with her." Ann wipes her eyes quietly so Belinda doesn't know she's crying. "I miss you, sweetie. Sleep tight tonight. See you maybe tomorrow evening, or in a couple of days, okay?"

I offer Ann my bed, but she insists I need my own familiar things about me. Therese pulls out her sleeping bag and some spare pillows from the closet, and Ann makes herself halfway comfy on the couch. I doze fitfully through the early morning hours and am stark awake by six o'clock. My mind scans and rescans the last twenty-four hours—and all that could lie ahead.

At eight thirty, after cups of coffee and half a cream cheese bagel each, the two of us are back in Jonah's ICU room. He's donned the purple boxers and video game T-shirt Vern has dropped off from his apartment. He looks like he's just come out of the shower. Even his toenails are clean. The three of us get into a long-drawn-out hug, then he scoots over so I can settle beside him on top of the covers.

"They let you shower?" I ask him.

"Strictly off limits. No, I got blanket-bathed—one of those ICU specials. Suze, my nurse, even washed my hair. God, I love my nurses." He grins. "Did you guys get some sleep?"

"An hour or two. It was tough switching off." I muster a smile and we bump noses. "You look like you got some shut-eye."

"Yeah, some. I watched twenty minutes of this dumb movie, which put me straight out. But you know hospitals—right after I'd dozed off there was an emergency—bells and beepers right out in the corridor. Next thing the night nurse was all over me checking my vital signs. Repeat procedure every couple of hours. Had to be sure I was still breathing."

There is a firm double-tap on the door and Dr. MacIsaac pokes his head in. He's carrying a beige file in his hand with several bits of paper sticking out.

"Morning, Jonah. Morning, you two. I hope you got some sleep."

"A little," Jonah tells him. "You were right, though—about waiting till morning to talk some more."

"Are you up for chatting about things some more?"

Jonah exchanges glances with us. "We're all ears, Doc."

"Okay, so the first thing to say is—though your cancer has definitely come back, it's at a very early stage. And the Decadron we're giving you, along with your anti-seizure meds, are keeping everything under control right now." He lays his file on the bed at Jonah's feet. "But we don't want to delay any more if we're going to get on top of this thing again. I've brought you a bunch of information about possible courses of action. Different treatment protocols."

"Like you gave me before?"

"Something like that, yes. But the chemo drugs we used before almost certainly wouldn't work if we tried them again. The cancer cells have become resistant to them, which is why it's growing again."

"But you're not entirely sure they won't work a second time around?" I press him.

"No, you're right, I can't be certain. The only way to know would be to simply go the same route again and see what happened. It comes down to—I hate to put it like this, but it comes down to making our best guess. You see, we have newer treatments that we think have a better chance of working. Because Joe's cancer cells have never been exposed to them, so they haven't had a chance to build up resistance. Okay?"

"Okay," Jonah said. "What about these treatments?"

"Well, there's a drug we didn't give you before. It's called Temodar, and you can take it by mouth as a capsule. In fact, it was almost the first drug that was found to work against your kind of brain cancer."

"Why didn't you use it before?"

"Good question, Joe. The simple answer is that the combination of drugs we did give you has shown more promising results lately. This drug

Temodar is becoming more of a second-line treatment. But it doesn't have such bad side effects as the chemo we gave you first, so that's in its favour."

"How good is it? I mean, how likely is it to cure me?"

Dr. MacIsaac stays silent a long moment. "Joe, I've got to tell you, the chances of it curing you are very small. The best thing we can hope for is to give you some time—many months, just possibly years. Which will give us cancer docs time to come up with more effective therapies that do have a chance of curing you. There's a whole lot of research going on in the bigger medical centres."

I'm finding it hard to come up with more questions. I take my journal out of my backpack, hoping it will help if I take notes—something I'm super-good at. But Jonah and Ann aren't holding back. Ann picks up the questioning from Jonah.

"This new drug you're talking about, how likely is it to work at all?"

"There's a fifty-fifty chance it will shrink Joe's cancer. And that response could last for a year or more. But there's no certainty about it."

"All right," Jonah intervenes, "so what else have you got to tell us about?"

"Well, there is another drug we can give you. It's called Avastin. It's quite different from most chemo, because it doesn't kill cancer cells directly. What it does is stop new blood vessels growing that feed the cancer. We would give it to you as an infusion, like with your earlier chemo. And it has more side effects than Temodar. Actually, we could give you both these medications together, but I can't tell you if the benefits of doing so would be greater than the harm they might cause."

Jonah stares unblinking at Dr. MacIsaac, avoids glancing in our direction. "But what you're telling me, Doc, is that none of this stuff is going to cure me, right?"

"I'm not saying that for certain, Joe. One thing I've learned going around the block so many times is never to make for-sure predictions. I have a handful of patients out there in the world who I never expected to make it."

"A handful?"

"Yes, I'm not saying a whole lot of people I've treated have defied the odds. But it definitely happens. There have been studies about it. About people with advanced cancer who had long remissions or were cured. No one's ever come up with a good explanation. Some people think it depends on attitude. I know you're not one to give in easily, Joe, and you're young— younger than most patients that get your kind of cancer. That likely counts in your favour. But when researchers studied these unexpected cures they couldn't find a clear pattern. Lots of people have very positive attitudes, so why weren't they cured?" He stops and changes tack. "Have you read much philosophy?"

"Yes. It's my minor. I love it."

"There's a saying of Kierkegaard's I love to tell the medical students. 'Life is a mystery to be lived, not a problem to be solved.' It keeps us doctors humble to remember that. It doesn't mean we won't solve this particular mystery, just that we haven't yet."

"I can live with that, Doc," Jonah says.

I find my voice. "Dr. MacIsaac, I want to say something. It's hard for me to take all this in, even though I've written down everything you've told us. And I know Jonah won't make any definite decision till he's talked to his mom and me. We all need a little time."

"And you haven't come right out and told us exactly what you recommend," Ann adds.

"You're absolutely right." The doctor lifts his file off the bed and takes out several sheets of paper. "What I have here are details of the possible treatments we've talked about. Just like when we gave you your initial chemotherapy. I want you to read them over so you can get a clear grasp of everything I've told you. In the end it's Joe's decision, but I know he's going to look to you both to help him. And you know what, there is no absolute right or wrong." He studies each of us in turn. "If you come back and say you want me to decide for you, that'll be absolutely fine. I'll do just that. But you should definitely take whatever time you need."

"Does Jonah need to stay up here in the ICU?" Ann asks.

"It would be best for now. Especially if we're going to be giving him new drugs." He leaves the papers lying on the bed as he stands up. "They'll call me right away whenever you're ready to talk more."

Twenty-Five

Jonah starts talking as soon as Dr. MacIsaac takes off.

"I'm not about to give up. I don't need Dr. MacIsaac to decide for me. He's talked about two new drugs, even said I could get them together. After what I went through before, I can handle whatever they dish out."

I pull myself up onto the bed beside him and Jonah wraps his good arm around me. I rest there for a long moment before saying anything, making sure I have my emotions under control.

"I know you can do it, Jonah," I say at last. "I'm so proud of you."

"I am too, Jonah," his mother adds. "But I think we need to read through everything he's given us, so we'll all know what to expect."

"You're right, Mom, but you know what? It won't make any difference, whatever's written there. I've got to go ahead. I owe it to myself—and to you guys. To all of you."

"Your mom and I can read this stuff together," I say. "Just like when you first got sick. Then we can tell you the basics of what you need to know."

"That'd be good, babe." He squeezes me tighter against him and whispers, "I love you."

We take off when Suze appears with Jonah's meds and a change of bedclothes.

"We'll look after him, no worries," she reassures us. "Nothing else is going to happen today. You two need to get some rest."

My eyes fill with tears at the nurse's tenderness. I quickly follow Ann out the door. We get no farther than the hospital cafeteria, sit next to each other with bowls of chicken and barley soup and cups of coffee. I read quietly to Ann from each brochure.

"It seems like the one he would get by mouth—Temodar—has been used especially for Jonah's kind of cancer. Its main side effects are stomach upsets and losing his appetite. But the Avastin gets used for all kinds of cancers and has a lot more side effects. It's pretty new, it sounds like. Dr. MacIsaac said he could give them both at once, so I guess Jonah could handle it. He'd have to be in the hospital each time, but we've been there before and got through it."

"How long would he have to be on the chemo this time? Does it say?"

"It looks like he would get the Avastin every few weeks, but I don't see where it says for how long. That's a question for Dr. MacIsaac, but I'm sure Jonah would get more scans fairly early on to see how it's working."

The oncologist shows up early the next morning to hear what we've all decided, and Jonah gives him the go-ahead. The intravenous drug is up and running by that afternoon, and Jonah swallows his first dose of Temodar. He doesn't ask the doctor anything more once he's told him what he wants to do. Dr. MacIsaac leaves it open about how many rounds of chemo Jonah will be getting.

"When it comes to a recurrence of your cancer, Jonah, we don't set any definite time limits on how long we continue. It will very much depend on how effective it is, and how you are handling it. We're looking at a couple of months before we do another MRI scan."

Jonah has a rough night. He starts vomiting late in the evening and can't keep even liquids down, despite the anti-nausea meds they are adding to his IV. They step up his IV fluids to keep him hydrated, but I'm shocked at how pale and washed out he looks when we arrive in the morning. He pulls himself up in the bed and summons a weak smile.

"Hope it's not always going to be like this. I guess this new stuff takes some getting used to."

Things settle down over the next few days, then they stop his intravenous Decadron and anti-nausea meds and move him back to a private room on the pediatric ward. Belinda brings Sophie up to visit on the weekend, and the two of them manage to hold it together, at least while they're spending time with Jonah. Then Bill and Dawn come by to perform a mini concert, which proves a big pick-me-up for everyone. Dr. MacIsaac says Jonah is stable enough to go home until the next IV chemo is due in two weeks. High time for me to decide if I'm up to writing my final exams. I've somehow found time and energy to study off and on, and I know I've got to try. I'll feel I've failed myself if I don't.

"I'll give Dr. Goldmann a call to let her know what's happening," the oncologist says. "But don't hesitate to get in touch with me directly if you want to talk about anything."

I worry about sharing Jonah's bed, but he tells me he won't hear of any other arrangement.

"I couldn't sleep a minute with you in that box room next door. And you'll be nice and handy if I need anything in the night."

He manages a wink as he says this, though I think privately that our sex life will be on hold for a while.

The next round of Avastin is even worse. Jonah had taken the Temodar religiously each day while he was home, even though it mostly left him sick to his stomach and antsy about swallowing anything more than the odd snack. Ann has talked to the hospital dietician about how to deal with Jonah's reluctance to eat anything but toast and the odd boiled egg. The dietician told her they used to recommend the BRAT diet— bananas, rice, applesauce, and toast—especially for children with bad tummy upsets. But it's out of favour because it's so bland and lacking in nourishment, even if it is gentle on the stomach.

"Joe needs to get some protein into him. Things like baked chicken and steamed veggies would be great. Eggs and cheese and nuts are good, too, and most yoghurt brands have a high protein variety nowadays, if he can stomach it. Small amounts of food around the clock are always the best way. With plenty of water or juice to wash it down each time."

Jonah does his best with all these instructions, but his taste buds are badly blunted by all the chemo he has received, and the less he eats the harder it is for him to build an appetite. I have all kinds of great nutrition ideas from when I worked at the health food store, but I mostly keep my mouth shut so as not to gang up on him. He and Ann come as close to falling out as I've ever seen them.

"Mom, I've got the message, okay? And I'm doing the best I can," Jonah says, playing with a small blob of scrambled egg and a single slice of lean bacon as Ann hovers nearby. "Can you back off a little and let me do this my way?"

By the time we get back for his third infusion of Avastin, Jonah has lost several more pounds and needs both Ann's and my help making it up to the ward from the parking lot. He's already wanting to barf in the bathroom before he gets settled in bed. I know the idea of no set limits on this chemo has got into his head. Or maybe it's just the whole hospital scene. Definitely not the way this man of mine had planned to spend the twenty-third year of his life.

The same goes for me. I'd never tell Jonah, but I'm secretly relieved when nine o'clock rolls around each night and it's time to head home to my apartment. Therese is spending most nights at Vern's place, but she makes a point of coming by Jonah's room with Vern to make some quiet music.

It's the one thing that lifts his spirits, and it gives Ann and me blessed relief from being the only faces Jonah sees all day other than hospital staff. The choir has also made a playlist of his favourite tunes that I've saved to his smart phone. He tells me it's great to listen to at night when he can't sleep.

Ann and I don't want to stock up with groceries when we're only staying in Halifax a few days each time. We get in the habit of grabbing supper at a quiet restaurant a block from the hospital before hitting the sack. Ann insists on picking up the tab each time. Dr. MacIsaac sets up another MRI scan before Jonah is due his fourth round of Avastin. They should be able to tell if it's working by now, he tells us, even though it's still early days.

"But we won't start the next chemo round till I've had a chance to go over the scan with the radiologist. If everything looks good, I'm thinking to cut back the doses of the chemo some. I don't have to tell you, Jonah, what a hard time you've had with it."

But everything does not look good. The doctor shows up within an hour of Jonah getting back from the scan. I know it's a bad sign that he's let so little time elapse. Jonah is dozing and Ann and I are chatting quietly in the window seat, trying to keep each other's spirits up. Jonah rouses as soon as Dr. MacIsaac appears. The doctor speaks without preamble.

"Joe, I'm very sorry to tell you this, but there's been a definite growth in your cancer. It's spreading backwards from where we saw it on the scans earlier. Not much, maybe no more than a centimetre or so, but it means this drug combination is just not doing its job."

I can't trust myself to speak, or even to move to Jonah's side. I cling to Ann's hand while Jonah holds the doctor's gaze. He's also silent. Dr. MacIsaac goes on after a long pause.

"Joe, this chemo has been very, very hard on you. And I don't think there's any point in keeping going with it. It would definitely have started to work by now if it was going to. We do have other medications we can try, but—"

Jonah interrupts him. "But you've given it your best shot, right? Or shots. Like, if any other drugs were any good, you'd have used them sooner."

"Yes. Yes, that's pretty much it, Joe. Of course, I will absolutely give you different chemo if you decide you want to go that route. It might keep things under control for a while, but I can't offer you more than that. And to give it any chance of working, you'd need to stay in the hospital and receive weekly chemo doses."

"How come I'm not having more effects from the cancer growing? I'm pretty weak, sure, but that's because I've eaten frig-all in the last couple of months. I'm not, like, paralyzed on the other side, or getting blinding headaches or whatever."

"Well, the good part—if there is a good part—is that there's some space up there where the cancer is growing. It hasn't started to press on any other vital parts of your brain or caused any more pressure build-up."

"But it might soon, right?"

"Yes, it might. We can put you back on regular Decadron by mouth— though it can have its own side effects when you take it long term. But it'll help to keep the pressure down."

Ann speaks up. "I know it's Jonah's decision, but what do you think? I mean, what would you do if it was *your* son in that bed?" Her voice breaks and she doesn't continue.

"I've been asked that question a good few times, Ann. And I have to tell you, I just don't know what I would do. I'm not where you are—where Jonah is. The only thing I know, I would wait until I'd had enough time to take this all in and talk to the whole family." He turns back to Jonah. "Maybe you'd like to stay here in the hospital tonight, so we can chat some more once you've all had a chance to get your head around things."

Once Dr. MacIsaac has gone Ann and I gather close on each side of Jonah's bed. None of us says anything until Jonah breaks the silence.

"I know I always said I was going to beat this thing. Well, that's still true—but it's in a different way from how I meant it before. I'm still going to beat it, but what I mean is, I'm not going to just lie down and give up. I'm still breathing in and out, I've still got life in me. I want to enjoy my time with you guys. In whatever ways I can, and for however long I've got."

I try to stifle the sobs rising out of my chest, but I do a lousy job of it. Jonah reaches to pull me in close.

"Babe, you don't need to pretend. You've got a lot of crying to do. Maybe I do too, I don't know. Neither of us is exactly the strong silent type."

I rest my head against his chest and let the tears flow as he holds me.

Twenty-Six

April

"I think we should head home and break the news to Belinda and Sophie," Ann says, once I emerge from the bathroom after freshening up. "I don't feel like telling them what's happening on the phone. And things aren't moving too quickly, Jonah, so you have some time to decide what you want to do."

"Okay, so what do you both think? Move in here and go for the big guns he's talking about?"

We're both silent, then I say, "I think your mom's right about going home, Jonah, at least for a bit. But let's talk to Dr. MacIsaac and get the full scoop. I mean, about what are the chances of different chemo working. And how many weeks in the hospital is he talking about?"

The doctor shows up the next morning holding a sheaf of papers with a familiar look. More drug protocols, more consent forms. Jonah starts right in.

"We're going to take off home, Doc—for a bit, anyway. See what some home cooking can do for me. It sounds like I have some time to decide on getting more chemo—or not." He fishes around for the piece of paper he's laid on his bed with some questions we'd all come up with. "This is what I want to know. Some of it anyway. How likely is it that any more chemo will work? And what's it going to do to me?"

"Those are big questions, Joe. And I'm glad you want straight-up answers—not everyone does. Well, I've had a chance to talk to some colleagues, both people I work with right here and a couple of doctors in other centres whose opinions I trust. The first thing to say is that your kind of cancer, at this stage, just isn't going to go away."

"It's incurable?"

Dr. MacIsaac holds Jonah's gaze a long moment. "Yes, that's right."

Jonah drops his head to the list of questions on his knee. "And it won't respond to the chemo I've had so far. What is any new chemo going to do for me? What's the best I can hope for?"

"More time is the most likely thing. Though even that isn't certain. As I said earlier, we always use the best drugs first. And the fact is, Joe, the cancer started to grow back only a few months after the first chemo we gave you. Then our second combination didn't work at all. I have to tell you that brain cancers often don't respond too well to our drugs. It may have something to do with them not penetrating as freely into your brain as they can other places. And brain tumours don't grow as fast as many cancers do. It's the fast-growing ones that respond best to chemotherapy. It's a long shot that any other drugs are going to do a whole lot of good."

"Okay, then how much harm will it do? It sounds like I'd have to be in the hospital for a long spell, right?"

"Right."

"And you'd have to give heavy doses if it's going to work at all."

"Yes. You're young, but you've soaked up a lot of chemo in these last few months—and it's had a pretty devastating effect on you."

"Yeah, it stinks. I dread every trip here." Jonah stops talking, avoids looking at Ann and me. "What if I decide not to get more chemo?" he asks finally. "What's going to happen then?"

"You don't duck the tough questions, do you?" The oncologist glances over at us. "How are you two holding up?"

We eye each other. "We're doing okay," I say. "We need to hear everything too. And two heads—well, three heads—are better than one when it comes to deciding what's next."

"Right. This isn't just Joe's illness. Cancer affects the whole family. Perhaps especially when it's a young person with it. Well, this thing isn't growing fast, like I said. And most of how Jonah's feeling right now—which is lousy—is because of all the chemo his body has had to soak up. Just being home and not getting bombarded with our drugs is likely to be a big help. Home cooking, like you said, Joe."

"If we decide no more chemo, you won't be my doctor anymore, right?" Jonah asks.

"Hey, I'm not going to just sign off on you! I'm your doctor, one of them anyway, and not just your chemotherapist, okay!" He pauses to make sure this sinks in. "You know, cancer—especially in young guys like you—isn't an everyday occurrence, so my patients come from big distances. And it helps I know your family doctor pretty well. You can come back to see me for check-ups any time, too, maybe get follow-up scans to see what's happening in there."

Ann poses her own question. "Dr. MacIsaac, I think Jonah wants to know—we all do—just what's down the line? If we need more help than our family doctor can offer us? Along with you on the phone?"

"You know about palliative care, Ann?"

Ann nods. "Yes, our local hospital has a palliative care team—though we've never had to call on them."

"I've worked with them a good bit," Dr. MacIsaac responds. "They do wonderful work. And nowadays we like to involve them quite early on. Not wait till—"

"Not wait till I'm in diapers and taking my last breath?" Jonah finishes the doctor's sentence.

"Yeah, that *is* what I mean. They can offer all kinds of support. Not just to you, but your whole family. You've got a younger sister, haven't you?"

"Yes, and she's taking things pretty hard. My other mom isn't doing too great either."

"I think it would be good if I gave your local palliative care team a call—as well as Dr. Goldmann. Whatever you decide about more chemo. Then the palliative care folks can meet you all and get to know you. The last thing I want to say, Joe, is deciding not to receive more anticancer drugs does not mean you're giving up. You know, a lot of people with cancer—too many, I sometimes think—just keep on going with treatment long after it's stopped doing them any good. Then they end up stuck in hospital because they're too sick to go home. You can think of it as taking back your life. Making your own decisions to have the best life you can every day. And enjoying every moment, however small. Whatever the future holds."

"That's pretty much what Jonah told us earlier," I say. "Thanks for talking to us all so honestly."

Twenty-Seven

The five of us gather around the kitchen table—the family meeting place. We three hadn't talked much on the drive home. I'd sat in the back with Jonah, holding his hand while he dozed off and on. Ann had called Belinda at work to say we were on our way and she'd give her the full scoop once they were together. I could hear the fear in Belinda's voice on the phone, sensing the news was bad. But Ann didn't try to simply reassure her. Her wife would have to face reality soon enough. The big thing was to offer the support of her own presence to Belinda and Sophie while she left it to Jonah to break the immediate news.

Jonah has taken up position at the top of the table. Belinda and Ann are on one side and Sophie and me opposite them. He looks at each of us before starting in. I marvel, not for the first time, how he manages to stay so calm—at least on the surface. I hope he won't be that way with me once I get him alone. It will be very hard, but I know I'd rather deal with the real Jonah, showing his true feelings—however scared and sad we both are.

"Dr. MacIsaac gave us the straight scoop right after I had my new MRI. The chemo isn't working. He said the scans would have told him for sure if it was doing any good."

Belinda immediately starts shaking, then bursts into tears. "Oh, Jonah, no! No!"

Ann wraps her arm around her shoulders. I reach out my hand to Sophie under the table. She grasps it tight, the features of her face fixed in a mask. Jonah says no more. Belinda turns into Ann and continues sobbing. I reach with my other hand to grasp Jonah's, only to realize I'm sitting on his left side. He's barely able to respond with his own squeeze. A squeeze that is already weaker than it was a week ago.

My heart stalls. I close my eyes, work to slow my breathing. To suppress the overwhelming urge to scream aloud at the injustice of it all. How could this be happening to the man I love so much? How could it be happening to this family I am more and more a part of—almost as much as my own? I manage to conquer the impulse, sensing Belinda is on the verge of falling apart. Sophie too. Dr. MacIsaac was too right—Jonah's cancer is this whole family's cancer. I've had little chance to shed my own tears and fears since we got the news earlier in the day. How is any one of us going to stay strong and support the others?

Jonah starts talking again. "Okay, so the doc said he could give me new chemo drugs, see if he could put a check on the cancer. But…" He stops, maybe feeling he doesn't need to finish his sentence. Belinda turns out of Ann's arms, her tear-streaked face wearing a look of desperate hope.

"But *what*, Jonah? Of course you've got to get more chemo! You can't just stop treatment. It would be like…" She doesn't finish her sentence.

Ann speaks gently. "Giving up? Is that what you were going to say, hon? We talked about that. Dr. MacIsaac told us a lot of people in this situation go on getting treatment that just leaves them stuck in the hospital, getting more and more sick. And it doesn't do any good against their cancers at this stage." She turns toward her son. "But I didn't mean to interrupt you, Jonah. You asked him all the right questions, and everyone needs to hear his answers." She reaches her free hand across the table to her daughter. "I know this is terribly, terribly hard to hear, Soph. And none of us is in any kind of shape to deal with it."

All five of us have become physically joined: Belinda and Sophie through Ann, Jonah and Sophie through me. Jonah goes on. "Dr. MacIsaac told me the chances of different chemo doing any good were very low. I'd be stuck in that hospital the whole time, and likely get sicker than I was with the earlier stuff. But he said he'd go right ahead if that's what we all decided." He looks around the table. "But we don't have to settle anything tonight."

There is silence save for Belinda's sniffles, which she's doing her best to stifle. I feel the weight of unspoken questions, of dread suppressed. No one has much appetite for supper, and efforts to lighten the conversation peter out fast. We all retire to bed early, though there seems little prospect of a sound night's sleep. Jonah and I lie quietly together in the dark, saying little but comforted by each other's closeness.

"I love you, Ellen," are his last words before he falls into a restless slumber.

"I love you too."

As I drift off, I feel his fingers slide down to the curve of my hip and across my belly. We fall asleep with both our hands entwined in pubic down.

When I join Ann in the kitchen in the morning, I learn Belinda had wanted to call in sick and take the day off. But Ann persuaded her she'd be better off with something else to occupy her mind. Nothing new was going to happen today.

"I told her Jonah hasn't definitely decided against getting more chemo," Ann tells me. "I explained it was Dr. MacIsaac who suggested we take a few days at home while he made up his mind."

I have a strong feeling that, despite Ann's reassurance to Belinda, Jonah has indeed made up his mind. All the chemo he has soaked up has done nothing but make him sick almost to death. I'm not sure any of us can go through that again. I acknowledge to myself almost with relief that Jonah is done with chemo. I have a store of ideas for other therapies that could do more good than harm. I had taken the time to check into the natural health co-op before we left Halifax and had come away with several items and a lot of suggestions.

"One thing we don't try to sell you is "cancer cures," Briony the store owner had told me. "But there's a whole lot of other things to try. Especially to lessen any symptoms that crop up. There are all kinds of natural ways to relieve anxiety and sleeplessness, and stress in general. Massage and reiki and meditation are all tried and tested, and there are a lot of other relaxation techniques. The more Jonah can get out in nature and exercise the better. And of course, yoga stretches while focusing on deep breathing—you and he can readily learn that online."

"We're both part of a students' choir, and I've read a lot about music therapy," I tell her. "Some of the choir members have already been working with Jonah."

"Wonderful. And talking of therapies for the senses, a lot of essential oils work well too. I'm thinking of lavender and tea tree oils, which you can use as infusions, rather than putting on his skin. Aromatherapies can be great for the whole family."

"What about acupuncture? It seems like there are a whole lot of acupuncturists opening up clinics lately."

"Absolutely. Especially if he's in a lot of pain, or too nauseous to eat."

"That could well become a problem. Thanks. What about dietary supplements?"

"Ginger is a big help with nausea, in drinks or with meals. Lots of other things—omega-3, turmeric, melatonin, probiotics. They all have some data supporting them, though it's very mixed. But given your background, it would be well worthwhile doing your own research. Oh, and don't forget cannabis—a good number of physicians are coming around to using it as an appetite stimulant. And maybe for pain too."

I had made notes as Briony talked, then realized I'd taken up a good deal of her time.

"Huge thanks," I say as I leave. "This will give me lots to work with. D'you have a card in case I want to get back in touch?"

She hands me her business card and wishes me the very best of luck. I find myself humming the tune that had been playing in the background while we were talking. More a chant than a tune—a soft, low-pitched ambience that soothes and uplifts me. There always seems to be background music like this—nature, wind, running water, birdsong—in places where healing is the primary intent.

Mid-morning the phone rings and Ann answers. After she hangs up, she comes and sits with Jonah and me at the table where we're enjoying coffee and toasted cheese that he's found he has some taste for.

"That was Alan Curran, the social worker at the hospice."

"Hospice, eh? That was pretty quick," Jonah says.

"He just wanted to touch base, let us know they were there if we needed them."

"What d'you both think?"

I speak first. "I think it would be good to meet him, Jonah. Whatever you decide about the chemo."

Jonah stands, takes his plate and cup to the sink, and turns to face us. "I've decided. I'm done with it. I knew it as soon as we drove away from the hospital yesterday. It felt like a huge weight lifted off me. Chemo may work for some cancers, but as far as I'm concerned it's something the devil dreamed up."

Ann and I move so we are standing close on either side of him by the kitchen sink. He lets himself be wrapped in our arms.

"It's just…I don't want to let you all down. If you think I should get more chemo…"

"Jonah, you're not letting anyone down," his mother interrupts him. "You heard what Dr. MacIsaac told us. Don't think of it as giving up. Think of it as taking charge of your life."

"What about Mom? You heard her last night. No way she'll accept me not going back for more."

"We'll deal with that," Ann answers. "She just loves you so much, and she's never one to hold back on her feelings. That's probably good. I could maybe take a leaf from her book."

The three of us sit quietly, each lost in unspoken thoughts. None of us wanting to contemplate the future.

"I want you to call Alan back, Mom," Jonah says at last. "Maybe he can come out today. While Belinda's still at work and Sophie's at school. Might be easier."

"You're right, it might," his mom answers.

I know at once it will help Jonah—help us all—to have someone other than family to support us.

Twenty-Eight

Alan Curran arrives an hour later. He looks to be about forty, short and casually dressed, long hair tied back in a ponytail. He greets Jonah with a beaming smile.

"I'm glad you decided to meet me. A lot of people have a hard time doing so." He turns to Ann. "This isn't the whole family though, is it?"

"No. My wife, Belinda, is at work and Sophie, Jonah's younger sister, is at school. We didn't want to overwhelm you with too many introductions right off. It's just Jonah and me—and this is Ellen, Jonah's girlfriend. She's part of the family nowadays."

"Well, I hope I'll get to meet everyone in time." The social worker lays his backpack down in the hallway. "But this is more of a social call to introduce myself. Tell you a bit more about Causeway Hospice and hear from you about where you are with things." He is once more looking at Jonah as he speaks. "Whatever you want to share with me."

"Thanks. What do I call you, by the way?" Jonah asks him.

"Alan! The whole team uses first names. And I hope you'll feel comfortable if we use your first names too."

"Absolutely," Ann answers. "Let's sit in the kitchen. That's where we have most of our family get-togethers."

"I guess you know quite a bit about my situation?" Jonah says once we're settled. "That I've got this brain cancer, and it didn't respond to any of the chemo that Dr. MacIsaac has given me. I'm home now to decide if I'm going to try…I guess you'd call them experimental drugs. He pretty much told me he didn't hold out much hope they would work. I was just talking with my mom and Ellen and told them I don't want to go back for any more of that stuff."

"Got it. You haven't told Dr. MacIsaac yet, though?"

"No. I need to talk to my other mom and my sister."

"Where are you with Jonah's decision?" Alan asks, looking at Ann and me. I feel at once the directness of his gaze.

"Well, we haven't had a chance to talk too much," Ann says. "But I think we both agree with Jonah. And we'll support him whatever he decides. Right, Ellen?"

"Right. It's Jonah's decision." I glance up at Jonah, blinking hard and fast to stem tears. "But it will be good for Jonah, for all of us, to have someone other than family to talk to."

"Belinda will have a harder time accepting Jonah's decision," Ann adds. "She more or less came out and said so last night."

"That's how we can often help. Jonah's the one who's got the cancer, but every one of you is involved. And we're here for the whole family."

"Well, it's good to meet you, but I'm doing okay right now." Jonah looks at Ann and me "Actually, I feel good now I've made my decision. Those trips were getting to me in a big way. I'm just looking to exercise some, get my strength back, put some meat on my bones. Have some fun for a change. And Ellen's been learning a whole lot about natural therapies and supplements I can try."

"Maybe you could tell us a bit more about Causeway Hospice," Ann says. "I mean, whatever you think we should know."

"Sure. Well, it's great to know you're doing fine right now, Jonah. Like I said, I'm just here to introduce myself. I'll say first that palliative care is a special kind of care for people and their families who are living with an illness at an advanced stage. Our sole purpose is to offer the person with the illness, and their family, the best quality of life possible. We like the term palliative care, because folk often seem to associate hospice with taking your last breath. Fortunately, doctors like Dr. MacIsaac are making referrals much earlier than they used to." He pauses to take us all in before continuing. "Okay, so we have a physician in charge—Betsy Ormerod—as well as nurses and a bunch of volunteers. We're available twenty-four hours a day, seven days a week, should any one of you need us. Betsy can prescribe whatever meds you might need—for pain and so on." Alan looks back at Jonah. "You're a college student, right?"

"Right. I was due to graduate this year, but I guess that's pretty much on hold."

"I only ask because I was thinking you're maybe no stranger to weed, am I right?"

"Well, I'm not a stoner if that's what you mean. But yeah, I've had my share." Jonah grins at me. "Why d'you ask?"

"It's just that, with cannabis now legal here in Canada, we're finding it has a big role in palliative care. It's great for giving you an appetite, as you probably know. It can help you sleep, and it looks like it helps ease pains of different kinds. Dr. Ormerod—Betsy—can prescribe it in whatever dose you find works for you. Just so you know."

"Yes, the owner of the natural health co-op mentioned that to me," I say to Alan.

"Well, that's good to know," Jonah adds. "I might well be calling on you if my appetite doesn't pick up."

The social worker turns back to Ann. "Look, you said your wife may well have a hard time with Jonah deciding against more chemo. One of us would be more than ready to help with this—it's a situation we run into in many families. I mean, about not being able to agree on the best thing to do." He lifts his backpack off the floor and pulls out some brochures. "Here, these are for you all to look over. More stuff about our services and so on. Be sure to give us a call any time you need us."

I take off upstairs as soon as Belinda and Sophie get home, deciding I'd be best to give this conversation a miss. Jonah will tell me whatever I need to know. He comes up to his room a while later and sits beside me on the bed. We prop ourselves up on our pillows to talk.

"How did it go? I mean, it's not strictly my business but…"

"It's for sure your business, Ellen. Aren't you part of my family now?"

I hug him close, kiss him on the forehead, nose, finally mouth.

"Yeah, you're my second family now," I answer at last.

"It wasn't easy, let me tell you. Both Belinda and Sophie were crying a lot. And Belinda's having a very hard time believing there isn't some magic bullet out there that can get the job done. She didn't say as much, but I know she thinks I'm just giving up. She hasn't been in the hospital as much as you two, and I don't think she's got a clear picture of how bad it is."

"Well, I for sure know. And Ann does too. Maybe Belinda should talk to Dr. MacIsaac herself, get the straight scoop. She might be thinking you haven't got it right, what he said to you. Though there were three pairs of ears listening—and it was clear enough to me and Ann."

"Yeah, Ann suggested that. And Belinda said she'd think about it. But I think even hearing it directly from the expert will be very hard for her. It'll be like the last door closing."

"How about Sophie?"

"She'll be okay. I mean, she'll get through whatever it is that's going to happen. And I think that hospice guy—Alan—can probably help quite a bit, like he said."

After supper we cuddle in bed, and both sleep better than we'd expected. Neither of us is in the mood for sex, but I get the feeling that part of our relationship is by no means over and done with.

Twenty-Nine
May

Dr. Ormerod makes a visit to introduce herself. She brings one of the hospice nurses, Sky, with her. At least six feet tall, her lanky frame topped by unruly red hair, Sky dwarfs everyone in the room.

"I want you to know that I'm always available," Dr. Ormerod says. "But you won't be seeing me more than weekly—or even less if all's going well. But Sky will be checking in with you a lot more often. She won't tell you this herself, but she's the best palliative care nurse you could ever wish for."

Sky laughs. "That's my standard introduction from Betsy. I've ceased to be embarrassed. It was Betsy who taught me to respond to a compliment with 'Why, thanks for noticing!'"

She laughs some more, causing her ginger curls to shake and the host of haphazard freckles on her face to dance. The nurse's humour lightens the mood in the room.

"I'll remember that line," I tell her. "Just in case I ever get a compliment around here."

"Babe, you're the most gorgeous girl on the planet," Jonah says immediately.

"Why, thank you, sir, for noticing!"

Sky claps at my swift answer, which has everyone laughing.

"You can come any time, Sky," Ann says. "Things have been a bit gloomy around here lately."

"I try not to do gloomy too much," the nurse responds. "Merriment mends, I like to say."

"I told you she was good, right?" says Dr. Ormerod. "Now to other business. I'm going to prescribe a small dose of cannabis for you, Jonah. It's mainly to stimulate your appetite. It's ninety-percent CBD—that's the part that relaxes, helps you sleep, but doesn't make you high. A lot of people find it's good for their appetite too. It's the THC component that causes the munchies and gives you that craving for sweets and fatty things. It also gives you the high that a lot of people are after. But there's only a very small percentage of it in this prescription."

Taking a small dose regularly under doctor's orders works well. Jonah finds he's less anxious and he's sleeping better. Our sex life revives too, much to both his and my delight. With no outward signs of the cancer progressing, we both find the dread that had plagued us receding. I reflect on what this time would have been like if Jonah had decided to get more chemo. Sex would have taken a permanent hike, even sleeping together. But most of all, he would have been suffering all those physical and psychological miseries that had overshadowed the previous seven months.

We spend lots of time with Sophie, enjoying the woods and the beach with her. One evening we build a fire near the water and roast marshmallows as though we were at summer camp. As dusk closes in, Sophie looks at her brother.

"It's been so great hanging out with you. These chunks of time you've spent at home, especially this last week or two, have been the best."

Jonah shuffles over to his sister and the three of us get into a group hug under the early stars.

Early in May Jonah wakes with a severe headache and barely makes it to the bathroom before throwing up. I give him three Motrin from the bathroom cabinet, and he manages to keep them down with sips of water.

"It feels just like when the pressure was building up in my head before," he tells me. "Throbbing away, especially on the right here." He guides my hand and lays it over the fuzz of hair on his scalp. "Your hand feels good. I guess it could just be a migraine."

"I didn't know you get migraines, Jonah."

"I don't." He tries to summon a grin. "Anyway, maybe it'll settle down if I sleep a bit longer."

Once Jonah is settled, I go down to the kitchen to let Ann know. Belinda has already left for work and dropped Sophie off at school on her way.

"He says it feels like when the cancer started to grow back. Maybe we should phone your doctor. Or even Dr. Ormerod."

"Let's wait and see. Let him sleep while you and I have breakfast."

We sit over tea and hot buttered croissants without talking much. I realize I've been waiting for the other shoe to drop. Is this it?

Jonah gets himself up late in the morning but he's moving cautiously like he's scared the headache will hit again if he makes any sudden turns. Dr. Ormerod has told him he can safely double up on the cannabis, and it seems to help after a bit. He has enough appetite to eat most of a BLT.

"I don't want you saying anything to Belinda or Sophie when they get home, okay?" he tells Ann and me.

Ann agrees. "No reason to worry them unnecessarily. Time enough if we need to later."

But the next morning the headache is back in full force, and Motrin and the higher dose of cannabis aren't cutting it. Ann tells Jonah she's going to phone Dr. Goldmann, and he raises no protest. She leaves a message with the receptionist, but just after she hangs up the phone rings again. It's Alan from the hospice making his weekly check-in call.

"Your timing's good," Ann tells him. "Jonah isn't doing so great right now. This is the second day he's woken with a bad headache, and Motrin and cannabis aren't doing the trick. I just called our family doctor, but I'm not sure Jonah's up to sitting in her waiting room for any length of time."

"I'll let Betsy know. She should be able to come over within the hour."

"That would be good. Thanks."

Alan is as good as his word. Forty-five minutes later Betsy Ormerod is examining Jonah on his bed while Sky stands by me in the background. After a few minutes Betsy sits herself on the bed's edge.

"There's some pressure building up there," she says quietly. "Dr. MacIsaac told me that was what happened before."

"Right. He called it papilledema. Is that what you're seeing?" I ask.

"Yes, I'm sorry to say, that *is* what I'm seeing. I think it's time to get you back on Decadron, Joe. And it would be good to up your dose of anti-seizure meds. I'll write a script for oral morphine too—sounds like you need something stronger than Motrin and CBD." She pauses and looks at Jonah and me in turn. "I'll let Dr. Goldmann know, and she can certainly arrange for a scan at the local hospital to make sure. We can get the images from last time sent over from the university hospital, so you wouldn't need to make another trip up there."

"Yeah, that'd be good," Jonah says.

Two days later we make the short drive to the local hospital. Ann and I have agreed it's best for us both to go along for reinforcements, not just for Jonah but for ourselves too. Jonah has been unable to lie flat since the headaches started up, but he's already feeling better since restarting the Decadron, and he can lie down for the scan without much difficulty.

Betsy and Sky show up at the house mid-afternoon the next day. The doctor addresses Jonah directly once we're all settled in the living room.

"The scan confirmed what I suspected, I'm very sorry to say. I already talked to Dr. Goldmann, and she sent her very best to you all. But she said it would be fine for me to come chat with you about things."

"What does it look like?" Jonah asks.

"Well, I didn't bring any copies of the scan to show you. But it's growing into the healthy parts of your brain—more on the right than the left."

"Is that why my left side feels weaker again?"

"Jonah, you never told me," I interrupt, trying to keep my voice calm.

"I wasn't sure, babe. And I didn't want to worry you."

I feel the urge to yell at him for keeping me in the dark, but that's the last thing he needs. I glance at Ann who is looking silently at her son. If his mom can hold onto her emotions, it's the least I can do to keep my own in check. Time enough later for tears—though whose shoulder do I have to cry on? I don't want to burden Ann, and as for Belinda and Sophie—well, I just can't go there. I wish Therese was with me right now. Hers has been a steady and strong shoulder ever since Jonah first got sick. Then I become aware of Sky who has moved close to me and laid a hand on my forearm. I feel the calming presence of the nurse's touch and have a strong urge to wrap myself in her long arms.

"What happens now?" I ask Betsy after a lengthy silence. The doctor turns to Jonah.

"Let me ask you first, Jonah—how are you feeling? I mean physically?"

"Well, I've still got a dull ache up here"—Jonah places his good hand briefly on the crown of his head—"but it's a whole lot better. And like I said, I feel a bit weaker on this left side, but I'm maybe just second-guessing myself."

"There's a couple of things then, Joe. It'd be good to keep doing as much as you can for yourself. But don't try to be macho—ask for help when you need it. I'm going to increase your Decadron dose, and I suggest you start taking the morphine pills regularly. MS Contin, we call them. They're slow release, so they go on working for many hours—even days in some people. I'll start you on a low dose—fifteen milligrams twice a day. The big thing is, Joe, it's good to take them regularly, because if you let the pain build up, it's harder to get on top of it. And I'll give you a laxative because opioids can constipate. You don't need to be straining and building more pressure in your head."

While Betsy busies herself writing the new prescriptions, Sky asks Jonah if he has more questions.

"Is there anything else the morphine will do to me?" Jonah asks her. "Like am I going to get hooked on it?"

"You might find you're a bit sleepier. Keep as active as you can. But as far as getting hooked, well, that's maybe not too much of an issue."

"What d'you mean?"

Sky looks around at Ann and me, then brings her eyes back to Jonah.

"I think you're going to need to stay on morphine or a similar drug, and Betsy will probably increase the dose after a while. Because your symptoms aren't going to go away."

It's Jonah's turn to glance at us. "Okay, so how long…?"

Sky looks over at Dr. Ormerod. "Maybe that's one for you, Betsy," she says.

The doctor takes her time answering. "Jonah, people in your situation, they can have a lot of say in how long. There may be a few things you specially want to do. People you want to see. That kind of thing."

"I guess so."

Ann speaks up. "Dr. Ormerod—"

"Betsy, please!"

"Okay, Betsy, what am I going to say to Belinda, and Sophie? Belinda's going to be a basket case, and I'm holding on by a thread as it is."

"What time do you expect her home?"

Ann glances at her watch. "Any time now. I lost track of time."

"Why don't Sky and I stick around till they get here. Any chance of a cup of tea?"

"I'll take care of that," I say. "I don't need to be part of this conversation."

"I'll help you." Jonah gets up slowly and we head for the kitchen.

Thirty

We've all moved into the kitchen by the time Belinda and Sophie get home. Belinda takes in the scene, stands rigid in the doorway for a long moment, then hurries toward Ann. Ann wraps an arm around her as Dr. Ormerod starts to speak, and Belinda leans against her wife. Not for the first time, the difference in their heights strikes me. For all her diminutive size, Ann is the strong one in their partnership. Jonah is once more sitting at the head of the table, and Sophie has moved in between him and me.

"I'm Dr. Ormerod," she says to the two newcomers. "I'm from Causeway Hospice. Please call me Betsy. And this is Sky, one of our nurses."

"Hospice? You mean…" Belinda can't finish her sentence. She starts sobbing in Ann's arms. Sky stands behind Ann's chair and lays her hands on her shoulders. Jonah and I both reach for Sophie, and she grasps our hands tightly. She squeezes her eyes shut. Her breath is coming in quick gasps. Betsy Ormerod keeps talking slowly and gently, pausing as she goes over what she's already told the rest of us. It's hard to know if Belinda is taking anything in, but Sophie seems to hang on every word. The doctor avoids any further mention of "how long."

"Jonah tells me he's already feeling better," she says. "There's no reason to expect anything else to happen right now. Sky will check in each day to see if there's anything else you all need."

Sky looks around at us all. "Here's my cell number. Call me twenty-four-seven—don't hesitate. Even just to chat on the phone. My husband long ago got used to sleeping through phone calls and getting our eight-year-old ready for school in the mornings."

The nurse's voice tells me I can trust her every word.

After Betsy and Sky leave, Ann persuades Belinda to head upstairs to their bedroom. No one has touched the tea, which went cold long ago. Jonah and I cuddle Sophie between us, and she finally lets her tears flow. It seems to me that Jonah is the one holding the family together—maybe with a little help from me. An hour or two later Ann comes to check on the three of us.

"Belinda's taken a sleeping pill and she's finally dozed off."

We take turns hugging each other, then I volunteer to make sandwiches for supper.

"I'll give you a hand," Sophie says at once.

We find it helps having something to occupy us, and I'm warmed by Sophie's presence beside me.

"You heard what Sky told us," I say. "I mean about phoning for a three a.m. bawl on the phone. She means it—and it goes for all of us."

Ann and Jonah stay at the kitchen table talking in low voices. No one has much appetite for the food, and after more hugs we take ourselves off to bed. Jonah and I lie close beside each other. I reach to wrap my arm around him as he snuggles tight against my breast.

"How're you doing?" he asks, his words partly muffled by my body.

"I'm wiped, Jonah. I don't seem to have any tears left to cry. You?"

He moves his head so I can hear him clearly. "Okay, I guess. We've just got to take each day as it comes, right? Each minute, maybe."

I nod my head against his. "Betsy Ormerod isn't going to set any time limits. Like she said, you've probably got a whole bunch of people you want to check in with. Especially your dad."

"You're right, babe. At least I can talk to him on the phone. But Alberta's a long way away. Anyway, I don't think I could handle meeting him—I mean, the way things are."

I pull him tighter against me. "Oh Jonah, I know it's selfish, but I want to keep you all to myself. Right here, safe from harm." Suddenly the tears are back, and I let them drip down behind my ears rather than move to grab tissues from the bedside table. Jonah's breaths deepen. I lie still a while longer, then close my eyes and sleep. I wake a few hours later to a clear resolution in my mind.

"Jonah, I want to marry you."

I speak the words softly but clearly into the dark. There is no movement on the other side of the bed. Jonah is lying curled up with his back toward me, and I can't be sure if he's still sleeping. I spoon my own body around him.

"Jonah, I want to marry you," I say again, a little louder.

This time there's a definite stir. "Wha…? What d'you say?"

"I said I want to marry you."

Now Jonah rolls over as quickly as his body will allow and gazes blearily at me.

"Did I hear you right? You *can't* marry me—I mean… What kind of a husband am I going to be to you? And—for how long?"

"I mean it, Jonah. I want to be your wife."

He is lost for words for a long moment. I finally sense his lopsided grin in the dark.

"Anyway, it's the boy gets to ask the girl—or so I always heard it."

"Okay, so were you about to ask me?"

Another silence, then, "I guess not."

"Well then?"

"Ellen, I know Betsy wasn't about to tell me how long I've got, but it sounds like this thing is moving faster. I mean, who wants a marriage that lasts a couple of months or whatever?"

"I do! Or two days if it comes to that. Or—who knows—two years." I stop, feel the tears gather once more. This time I reach for the tissues. "I don't want us to sit around waiting for…I don't know what." I blow my nose, grab more tissues. "I want to have something to take our minds off everything,"

"Oh, so this marriage idea is just to give us something to do?"

I look at him sharply, can see in the rising dawn that the grin is still in place.

"You know what I mean! Oh, Jonah, none of us knows how much time we have. And I want to treasure every moment together. What better way than to have a wedding?"

Jonah wraps himself around me, draws me in tight, and kisses me, his lips pressed against mine for an endless moment. I love the fit of his body against my own. Exciting, and totally tuned to each other's. The whole country of his body has become familiar.

Finally, he draws his face away from mine. "Ellen Jane, will you marry me?"

"Jonah Daniel, I will."

Jonah rolls towards me, and with a good bit of help comes to lie fully on top. My last thought before instinct takes over is one of thanks that some parts of my husband-to-be's anatomy are still working fine. I lose the sense of where my body ends and his begins. Minutes later he is drifting back into slumber. I make no effort to shift his weight as I lie wakeful and sated beneath him, gazing out through the window at the lightening sky. At Orion and the Big Dipper gleaming overhead—as they have for a million years and will so continue for another million.

Thirty-One

Once everyone gets into the notion of a wedding, a sense of happy urgency fills the household. I talk to my mom and dad on the phone about bringing Jonah to their place to spend some time with them both before the wedding.

"I guess he's not coming to ask permission to marry my daughter?" Dad says a little ruefully.

"Mom told me you two snuck off and got hitched without anyone knowing, Dad!"

"When did you tell her that, Edie?" he asks my mom. They have the phone on speaker.

"Well, your parents were sure I wasn't the right one for you. We sure proved them wrong, honey."

"Sure did."

I warm to their voices as I listen to their chatter. "Well, you guys aren't going to have any doubts about Jonah and me," I tell them, then hesitate. "But we're setting an early date, and we're going to get married in Jonah's home."

I had told them all about my fiancé's situation, but I'm not sure if they've fully grasped the seriousness of it all. I'm hugely relieved by my mom's next words.

"Listen, Ellen, Dad and I have gone over everything you told us. We're deeply, deeply sorry, you know that. But we also know you don't want us dwelling on it. You and Jonah don't need any gloom and doom around you right now."

"But we want to make things as easy as it can be for you," Dad adds. "We've decided that once you've set the date, rather than you travelling here, we'll book a hotel near Jonah's home and come a few days before the wedding. That way we can get to know his whole family some too."

"And I can help with last-minute stuff," my mom says. "Dad will of course be giving you away. That's one tradition that's alive and well, even if your altar is a plant stand in the living room!"

I tell Ann and Belinda my parents' plans as soon as I get off the phone.

"That'll be just lovely," Ann responds. "The more the merrier—and it'll be a perfect way to meet them. Remind me what their names are?"

"Edie and Gerry. They're a couple of lovebirds. They'll be celebrating their silver wedding anniversary next year."

"Hey, there's a couple of lovebirds right here who aren't far short of twenty-five years married!" Ann giggles happily. "Okay, so down to business. I talked to the local justice of the peace, Will Croydon. He's done quite a few at-home weddings. Have you settled on a date, you two?"

Jonah and I look at each other. "We want to get our Songlines choir down here," I answer. "We thought we'd work around when they can all get away."

"And could you find out when Will's free, Mom?" Jonah asks her.

"Will do."

"Well, I want to buy you your wedding dress, Ellen," Belinda says. "That might take a couple of shopping trips."

Since Jonah and I announced our plans to get married, Belinda seems to have reached a place of calm, perhaps even acceptance of her son's situation. I notice she's going out of her way to spend extra time with Sophie. But we still hear muffled sobbing from his parents' bedroom, and we're pretty sure it isn't Ann—if anything she's too stoical.

"Wow, that would be wonderful," I say to Belinda. "But I don't want anything too formal or showy. And I'd like you to come too," I add, turning to Sophie who has just come into the kitchen.

"Come where?"

"On a wedding dress hunt! Your mom wants to take me shopping. And I need your input."

Sophie blinks hard and fast. "That would be awesome," she says huskily.

"Though it might be hard to find a dress we can all three agree on," I add, which brings a burst of laughter from everyone.

"There's no school tomorrow—teacher's meeting or some deal," Sophie says. "Could you maybe get off from work early, Mom?"

"I can do better than that," Belinda answers. "My boss is out of town till the weekend, so I'll take the day off! It'll be great to spend the whole day together."

The next morning the three of us try the two women's clothing stores Belinda has in mind, the second one specializing in wedding attire, but come away empty-handed. I try on a few outfits, but they're way too formal for the low-key ceremony Jonah and I have in mind.

"Are there any vintage clothing places in town?" I ask Belinda and Sophie.

Belinda looks blank but Sophie answers at once. "Yes! There's a fun place off Main Street—a consignment shop. My friends and I have been in there a couple of times."

The store is on two levels in an older building. There are even a few racks of clothing out on the sidewalk. As I push open the door, a dress hanging on the end of one of the racks catches my eye. It is crisp and silky-looking, and most of the colours of the rainbow are represented in its broad horizontal stripes from shoulder to mid-calf. It has long sleeves that expand out at the top. As I move to feel the fabric a voice speaks up. There's a woman sitting behind a desk largely hidden by clothing racks.

"Nice, isn't it? Yarn-dyed taffeta. And those are called Juliet sleeves. It just came in yesterday."

I lift the dress off the rack and hold it against myself.

"It's you!" Sophie exclaims at once. "Oh, go try it on! Quickly!"

Belinda smiles at her daughter's enthusiasm, then gazes at me with moisture gathering on her eyelids. The shop owner points toward a curtain at the back of the store.

"You can change in there."

I love the rustling sound the material makes as I pull it over my head. The dress fits almost perfectly, but when I look in the mirror it seems to me the waist is too loose, and I notice the hem is uneven, with one side hanging a little lower than the other. I swing the curtain back and step into the room, swishing the dress back and forth over my thighs. All three women look like they are about to burst into applause. Sophie is the first to speak.

"Oh, it's magical. You look gorgeous."

"It's a bit loose around here," I say, indicating the waistline. "And I think the hem's uneven."

"No, no, it's meant to hang like that." The shop owner comes out from behind the desk carrying a box of pins. "It looks very elegant on you—and very retro. Is it for a special occasion?" She inserts several pins to narrow the waist.

I blush. "Yes, a very special occasion. I'm getting married." As my tears well up, I glance over at Belinda and Sophie. Both of them are trying hard to hold back snuffles. I summon a smile.

"Oh dear, we're all pretty weepy today—and this is s'posed to be a joyful occasion," I say. "Well, I guess they're mostly tears of joy, right?"

Everyone smiles. "Right!" Belinda affirms.

"Well, congratulations!" the shopkeeper says. "And don't worry, you're not my first customers to have a good cry in here. Now, I think I can find you some shoes to go with that gorgeous dress. And how about a lacy veil to complete the look? Take a look around while I fix the waistline. The hem is just right—I'm not going to touch it. And I can make the alterations to the waistline in no time. My name's June, by the way."

Belinda spots an antique-looking lace shawl embroidered with flowers and leaves that will make a perfect veil.

"Chantilly lace," June tells us. "A hundred years old, maybe more."

She drapes it over my head and shoulders. "Just like a mantilla, though it's actually French, not Spanish." She suddenly breaks into song: *"Chantilly lace, and a pretty face, and a ponytail hangin' down."* She starts dancing on the spot and Belinda joins in. *"A wiggle in her walk and a giggle in her talk, make the world go round!"* Belinda grins at me and Sophie as we gape at these older women who have taken off for another planet. They do a high-five as they come to a halt.

"Jerry Lee Lewis," Belinda tells us. "I used to dance to it in the kitchen as a little kid. Wow, that takes me back—seventies music!"

"It was The Big Bopper first sang it," June says. "Way back in the fifties, I think. Long before *our* time, right?"

Once the two women have caught their breath, June lifts a pair of beige ballet flats from a rack of shoes. "I think these would work beautifully."

They're a perfect fit. Miraculous.

We browse around as June makes the alterations to the dress and wraps up the whole wedding trousseau. I give Belinda a big hug.

"I can't thank you enough. Everything is just lovely."

"And we all agreed right away," Sophie adds. "What was the chance of that? But won't you need a necklace or choker or something?"

"I think that's being taken care of," Belinda says quickly.

"Whoops."

"Right, whoops! I'll tell you later," Belinda wraps her arm around her daughter while grinning at me. As my soon-to-be mom-in-law settles the bill, I can't help noticing the lace veil has cost more than my dress and shoes put together.

All of the Songlines members, including Raig, can make it a week from Saturday, which turns out to work for Will Croydon too. The date is locked in. My parents arrive Thursday afternoon, and our two families enjoy a pre-nuptial feast of Ann's cooking washed down with flasks of sangria. Jonah drinks half a glass before I remind him of Betsy's warning: alcohol and opiates don't mix too well.

"Spoilsport."

"I'm sorry, I don't want to start nagging you before we're even married!"

"You nag? Never. I know you're just watching out for me, babe."

Ann drives Jonah and me to the justice centre the next morning to collect the marriage license. Jonah is growing progressively weaker on his feet, and I have to almost shoehorn him into the back seat.

"It's that bigger dose of MS Contin Betsy's put me on. It's working great for the headaches, but it's making me pretty woozy."

"Mixed with the sangria you glugged back last night," I say with a giggle. "One way to work up a hangover!"

Jonah looks at me as we sit in the justice centre with the certificate in our hands.

"Still sure you want to go through with this?"

"You kidding me?" I lean over and kiss him. "I love you, Jonah."

"I love you too, Ellen. Heart and soul."

He sleeps on my shoulder in the back of the car while Ann stops by the JP's house to deliver the signed certificate.

Our two families are busy the rest of Friday with last-minute preparations. I try on my dress for Mom and Ann in the bedroom. There are tears in both their eyes when I stand before them in my wedding attire, making swishing sounds with my skirt.

"You look utterly beautiful, Ellen," Ann says. "I'll never find words enough to thank you for deciding to marry my son. Knowing what we all know."

"I'm so happy for you both," my mom adds. "And proud that you're my daughter."

We join in a three-way hug, all giggling like teenagers as we set up more rustling.

"I never owned a taffeta dress," Ann says. "But at least now I know what it sounds like!"

She reaches into the pocket of the apron she is still wearing from breakfast, pulls out a small square box, and hands it to me. "This is to complete your ensemble."

Wrapped in cotton batting inside is a dark blue cameo locket on a silver chain. I open the clasp and smiling up at me are miniature photos of Jonah and myself side by side.

"Oh, it's gorgeous, Ann. Just perfect to complete my ensemble. Can you help me fasten it?"

She steps behind me and I reach my hands back with the two ends of the chain. "There," she says.

"It's just the right length," says Mom.

I move to the mirror. The pendant hangs down to just below my collar bone.

"That sneaky Sophie insisting on getting photos of Jonah and me the other day—she never let on what she was going to do with them!"

"The jeweler didn't know how old the locket is exactly," Ann says. "But it sounds like it might be as old as your veil."

"It's wonderful! Oh, and that reminds me—as soon as the shop owner draped the veil over me, she started singing this song I'd never heard before. About Chantilly lace."

"I'll bet Belinda joined in—probably started dancing too, right?"

"They both did—it was hilarious."

Mom immediately starts singing the lines I'd heard in the clothing store. "*Chantilly lace, and a pretty face, and a ponytail…*"

"I'm guessing you danced to it as a little kid too, Mom," I laugh.

She beams back at me, tears of joy making her eyes bright.

Thirty-Two

The seven choir members arrive in two carloads late Friday afternoon. Belinda has arranged for them to stay at a motel, Therese sharing a room with Raig, Vern with Bill, and Amy, Carole, and Dawn squeezing into a third. They gather in the kitchen for a pot of Ann's succulent chili, washed down with beer and some of her homemade red wine. Jonah is hugely cheered by seeing so many of his friends, all of whom offer boisterous congratulations to us both. There's a notable absence of comments on the change in his appearance. No one dissolves in tears, though Amy and Carole look like they want to. Once I've hugged and checked in with everyone, I drag Therese off to the living room sofa so we can do some proper catching up. It takes about two minutes for my tears to start flowing—a mix of seeing my best friend after too long and the bitter sweetness of the whole occasion.

The wedding is set for two o'clock Saturday afternoon, and our two families take their time over breakfast that morning. When I decide it's time for me to prepare, Ann looks at Belinda, then at my mom.

"Your mom and I are going to help you get ready, Ellen."

I love the way the moms have already come together to arrange things. I know my dad will have been thinking through exactly how to stage the giving away of his only daughter. I'm not even going to speculate what he's planning. I just know he will take charge once the moment comes to "lead me to the altar."

At one-thirty the Songlines choir starts singing several favourites, with Bill on the guitar and Vern on drums. Everyone gathers in the living room. Sophie the appointed wedding photographer is busy catching every moment.

There are plenty of flashes from cellphones as others grab the chance to mark the occasion. I'm sneaking a look from the kitchen where Dad and I are hiding. The three moms and Sophie, decked out in floral dresses, greet the additional guests as they arrive. Three of Jonah's friends from high school have come, each with a date. Betsy, Sky, and Alan from hospice and Will Croydon, the JP, complete the guest list. Jonah is kitted out in a dress shirt and bow tie, smart black pants, and shiny black shoes. His hair is starting to grow back and is all frizzy ends, but he's sporting a full beard.

On the chime of two from the hall clock, the door between the living room and kitchen swings open. My dad, dressed in a grey linen suit and flower tie, ushers me forward into the room. For a long moment before he takes my arm, I stand resplendent before the assembled company. There are several gasps, then everyone breaks into applause as I move to the centre of the room on my father's arm. Tears are now flowing freely all around.

"I don't think you're s'posed to applaud till after it's official," I offer amidst laughter as the clapping dies down. The choir break into Beyoncé's "Crazy in Love" as Bill strums, Vern drums, and my dad steps back to allow Jonah to move forward to my side. We grin happily around the room before turning to each other to say our vows. We begin with a Rumi poem that we speak in unison.

> The minute I heard my first love story
> I started looking for you,
> not knowing how blind that was.
> Lovers don't finally meet somewhere,
> they're in each other all along.

Jonah stumbles with the words a couple of times but keeps going. We finish with the short vow we've composed between us, this time speaking our words in turn.

"I love you, Jonah. I will be forever true to my mission of love and care for you, and for the world about us. I love you."

"I love you, Ellen. I will be forever true to my mission of love and dedication to you, and to everyone who loves and cares for us. I love you."

Will Croydon moves to stand in front of us as we hold hands. He speaks without notes.

"By joining hands, you are promising to honour, love, and support each other for the rest of your lives. By the authority vested in me by the laws of this province, I pronounce you husband and wife. I wish you both every good fortune, and it is my honour to introduce Ellen and Jonah to the assembled company."

This time there is sustained applause amid the popping of champagne corks. The choir bursts into their own version of Taylor Swift's "You Belong With Me," followed by Adele's "Someone Like You," and finally Stevie Wonder's "Signed, Sealed, Delivered." The wedding guests join in familiar parts of each song and even find small spaces to dance together. Mom has disappeared briefly into the kitchen and comes back with a huge array of peonies, yellow lilies and pink and white phlox, which she had hidden somewhere till that moment. She presents it to Jonah and me, then wipes her tears with a pretty lace handkerchief she draws from the sleeve of her dress.

The party spreads itself between the living room, hall, and kitchen for the wedding feast as Sophie snaps picture after picture. Jonah and I set about opening a selection of gag gifts that have been stacked on the sideboard. There are matching T-shirts emblazoned with "Trophy Wife" and "Trophy Husband"; baseball caps reading "Mr. Right" and "Mrs. Always Right"; thick wool socks with the message "In Case You Get Cold Feet"; Mr. and Mrs. toilet rolls; His and Hers underwear embroidered with obscene slogans; and coffee mugs with the inscription, "Keep Your Ups and Downs in the

Bedroom." There are cards from many of the hospital staff, including a gift certificate from Dr. MacIsaac. Dad whispers to me enigmatically that our wedding present will be arriving soon.

The party finishes up back in the living room. There is silence as Jonah takes a couple of sips from my champagne glass and thanks his family and friends. Then he takes from his pocket a small page of handwritten notes.

"Ellen, it was you who proposed to me—and I couldn't talk you out of it. I'm sure glad I didn't. Being loved by you is everything I could ever ask for. If I were to live a hundred years, I'd belong to you for each and every one of them. If I'm to die before you, every atom of me will keep searching till I find you again."

I gaze back, then murmur my own words to my new husband.

"You're my heart, my soul, and my life, Jonah. There will be something good in every moment we spend together."

Thirty-Three
June

I join Ann in the backyard to check out the early activities of the bees. The late spring weather has been warm and the songbirds are back. Early roses and peonies are replacing the hyacinths, tulips, and sweet daphne. Bees are foraging for nectar and pollen everywhere.

"They've consumed most of their winter stores of honey," Ann says. "They know to emerge once there's pollen and nectar to be had. Nectar for energy, pollen for protein." She busies herself with zip-lock baggies, almost filling them with syrupy liquid. "To supplement the bees' own foraging," she tells me. "I'll keep doing this every few days into summer till I'm sure they've harvested enough nectar and pollen to build their combs and see them through next winter."

She lifts each hive in turn to test their weight. "Tells me how much nourishment they still have left. Most of them are fairly light, so they'll need a good bit of supplement." She lifts the top off each hive in turn, pierces several holes in the baggies, and inverts them over mesh networks. "You have to be careful not to drown the bees. I've tried different ways, but this seems to work best. I give them protein patties as well, which I make from syrup and dry pollen and a few drops of lemongrass oil."

I love the peace and beauty of the backyard and the ancient instincts of the bees. I know how crucial they are—to the whole human race. Ann tells me that if every one of these tiny creatures were to die, human beings wouldn't survive either.

"There are all kinds of fruits and veggies that need bees to pollinate them so they can grow. Broccoli, cucumbers, tomatoes, blueberries, you name it. And a lot of commercial crops too—just to keep the cycle of life turning. I'm sure you've heard about the dropping numbers of bee populations. It's all those pesticides, as well as infections and loss of habitat. Everyone who has the space should probably keep a few hives in their backyard."

"I'll certainly plan to one day," I tell her. "But meantime I love learning about them—though it seems there's an awful lot to know."

"Oh, you'll do just fine. Bees are so smart they can build their own hives if they need to—look at all the wild bees out there. I remember when I first started, I left off the sides of one hive by mistake, and the bees simply built their own with beeswax. Complete with proper ventilation and temperature control!"

It has been three weeks since we scattered Jonah's ashes in the woods at the back of the house. I've kept back a part of the urn's contents so I can take it with me to my own home. My parents have gone along with my wanting to keep vigil for my husband here on the land where we spent our last few precious weeks together.

"Don't leave until you're ready," Mom had said on the phone last night.

"Thanks, Mom. I think I'll know when that is. It's like once I leave, I'm saying a final goodbye to Jonah. Not to his spirit, but to his earthly being." I realized I hadn't felt such a clear awareness before. I swallowed and blinked several times, glad my mother couldn't see me. "I know I'll be keeping in close touch with Ann and Belinda and Sophie. Probably visiting sometimes. But you're going to have me for the next good while. Until I know for sure what I want to do with my life."

"Are you certain about putting off medical school? Maybe indefinitely?"

"Yes, I am. It helped when I went back to see my dean. He talked about gap years, not committing myself till I was absolutely sure. He was nice enough not to mention my MCAT score. I'd have to put in a solid year's study to catch up with the competition. Anyway, I know I'm in no shape to make big decisions." I muster a small giggle down the phone. "You know, the first patient you have in med school is a dead one. Even the thought of dissecting a cadaver sends shivers through me."

My mom's answering laugh makes me realize this is the first time since Jonah's death I've managed to make a small joke. A death joke. Jonah would have appreciated it.

"It'll be great to have you home, Ellie," my mother says. "One unexpected plus from all this, we get to have our daughter back for as long as… well, who knows how long?"

I had been halfway through the arduous task of preparing application packages for five medical schools, giving myself time to have them looked at by my professors before the mid-July deadline. I knew I would be waiting to hear at least until late summer, especially if I got put on a hold list. Then it had finally come to me: I wasn't ready to face it. Medical school loomed like an immense mountain that I didn't have the capacity to climb. Maybe never would.

When I relive my memories of our precious three weeks of marriage—May 8, wedding day, to May 29, death day—it's painful and comforting both. There were more joyful moments than sad ones. Jonah and I lived deep inside each one of those days and nights. I can vividly picture each feature of his face—the dark of his eyes, the roundness of his jaw, the smoothness of his lips and neck.

We had made several trips to the nearby woods, where Jonah gave me more nature lessons. Taught me to distinguish trees by their bark, even a silver maple from a sugar maple and a white oak from an English oak. I think of the very last time we plodded toward home, toward bed, toward sleep. It had felt as if we were walking in the sacred tracks of those Indigenous Australians. Jonah woke one morning from a dream of wandering the songlines.

"Was I with you?" I asked him.

He turned his body into mine. "I could see you. But you couldn't see me."

We made a couple more trips to the market, and each time sold out of Jonah's cheese and garlic pretzels. At night we read to each other in bed until Jonah could no longer make out the words. Betsy Ormerod told me his failing vision was from the cancer pressing on his visual pathways, but the morphine was surely adding to it. The combination of the opioid and cannabis kept his headaches at bay but meant more and more sleepiness and wobbliness. Betsy acknowledged when I pressed her that the increasing doses of morphine were controlling his headaches—but yes, they were perhaps shortening his life too.

There came a time when Jonah couldn't make it to the bathroom, and Sky suggested diapers. He was eating and drinking less and less, so it wasn't a big deal to change him. Jonah had managed to joke about it—"It's not dying I mind, but p-p-p-lease, not in diapers!" But the nurse quickly convinced him it would be a lot easier on all of us.

"We're all born into diapers, and most of us die in them. Hopefully with someone to switch them out when needed," she'd said.

As I sat at his bedside, my hands would often go to the chain fastened about my neck. I had an immediate image of Jonah, the way he looked when Sophie took his photo for the locket. That smiling image was much easier to remember than my very last one of him. Watching his breath growing fainter and fainter, the colour of his hands fading to white, then to dull blue, his heartbeat finally fading to memory as he drifted into the warm womb of death. As I'd leaned in to kiss his lips for the very last time, I had felt no familiar answering breath on my face. It was like connecting with his aura.

In the days leading up to that last moment, I massaged his wasted body in the gentle rhythmic way that Sky had taught me. The nurse suggested I experiment with different oils, and I'd settled on a mix of lavender and peppermint, which always soothed Jonah when he was especially agitated. Sky told me peppermint has strong analgesic properties, and Jonah said it lessened his headache when I massaged his forehead and temples. I myself found inhaling the aromatic oils calmed me too.

Sky talked about what she called music thanatology. "We learned a few years back that harp music and chanting can be soothing to our patients. There are musicians who get professional training in it, but recorded music works well too. I've created a playlist for you to download."

After that, the sounds of harp music and monastic chanting often filled the room, and the whole family took joy in it. The lines of Jonah's face would relax, and he'd mostly fall into a peaceful slumber as the music played. Once he opened his eyes and told us sleepily, "Comfort food for the ears."

Ann and Belinda and Sophia would take turns sitting with him so I could catch a few hours' sleep in Sophie's room. Sky showed us all how best to roll him from side to side, change his sheets and pillowcases without disturbing him, and clean his gums with lemon and glycerine swabs. Jonah took a particular liking to frozen ginger popsicles, and Ann kept a regular supply in the freezer.

As it became clear the end was coming, I stayed by him round the clock, with the family checking in for short intervals and bringing me snacks of food and drink. Sky was there a good part of each day and often well into the evening.

"He hasn't had a thing to eat for days," I said at one point. "He's not even swallowing fluids. He must be hungry for something—or at least thirsty."

"I don't think Jonah is feeling much hunger or thirst at this point," the nurse answered. "People used to think we should give IV fluids when patients stopped drinking. But artificial hydration isn't necessary or even beneficial. The important thing is to keep his mouth clean and moist."

There was a peaceful quality to the silence that followed Jonah's final breath. The moment when I leaned in to kiss his eyelids, cheeks, lips, for the last time. Sky had been right beside me that whole night. She'd been at the house for the last forty-eight hours, with interludes to head home for an hour or two to check on her husband and daughter. She would kneel down at Jonah's bedside to tend to him—in the ancient attitude of prayer. She and I had shared life stories while the rest of the family slept. It was only much later that I took note of the time typed on the death certificate: 4:15 a.m. I had dozed off in my chair when Sky laid a gentle hand on my arm to tell me it could happen at any moment.

Sky told me that many, perhaps most, people died at night. "That's why I'm a night owl," she said. "It's almost as if they take their loved ones' sleeping as permission to enter their own eternal slumber."

Looking back, I can see how Sky fit the role she'd been trained for. Aware and caring instantly for all Jonah's bodily needs, watching out for all of us. Answering our questions, guiding, teaching, consoling, even lightening things up when the chance arose. Most especially, she imbued a tireless and loving presence. A spiritual presence.

Toward the end, while he was still clear and coherent in his mind, Jonah told me and Ann and Belinda that he wanted to be cremated and have his ashes scattered in the forest where he and I had found so much joy and solace. After his cremation we took turns to spread a handful of ashes, then held a silent vigil for several minutes, shared a group hug, and walked home under a canopy of overarching maples and oaks.

Sky and Alan continued to visit afterwards. Alan mentioned that some people found it helpful to write letters to their beloved dead. I'd been keeping a journal of memories of Jonah, to be sure I didn't forget any of our precious moments together. It was easy to turn some of those scribblings into a letter.

Sweetheart,

You're in my thoughts every waking moment. You said on our wedding day that every atom of you would keep searching till you found me again. And now that you're gone, well, I shall never stop searching for you. We've scattered your ashes in the woods like you asked. Except a small portion I kept back to take with me to my own home. But I know that something of you still exists. Somewhere out there, or—better yet—somewhere deep inside me. We're still two souls cozied up together.

I've decided I'm not going to try for med school after all. I'm still not sure what I'll do, but it will be caring for people, that's for sure. I will always wonder what you'd have done with your life. Whether you'd have gone on and done your Ph.D. in anthropology like you talked about? Or maybe you'd have become a chef! You had such a natural gift in the kitchen, just like your mom.

They're all doing okay, by the way—ups and downs of course, all of us, but we're helping each other make it through each day. I'm keeping in touch with our Songlines buddies, especially dear Therese.

One thing about your whole illness, Jonah—it's brought so many loving and caring people into my life. There's nothing I'd rather do than give back some of that loving and caring. The nights are lonely, though, Jonah. If it's good to cry, like they say, well I should be doing very well with the number of nights I've soaked our sheets with tears. I still think I can smell you in those sheets.

Alan was right—it's been a lovely comfort to write to you. I love you, Jonah. Like the song says, I'll hold you for a million years—and maybe in time you can teach me how to live without you.

Your loving wife, Ellen

I've now written a stack of letters to Jonah and stored them safely in a drawer in our bedroom. Who knows, perhaps one day I will get an answer from him. A rather stilted phrase comes into my mind that I'd read in some Victorian novel: *I am expectant of your early reply.*

I phone my parents again. It's my father who answers. "Dad, I'm ready to come home. It'll be a perfect test run for my wedding present. I've hardly taken it out since Jonah died." The gently used silver-grey Ford hybrid had been sitting on the driveway when my mom and dad took me and Jonah out for a breath of fresh air once the wedding party had broken up. They'd purchased it from a local dealer and had it delivered just before they left Ontario.

"Wonderful news, Ellie. Take your time and drive safely."

"I will, Dad. I'll see you Friday late afternoon, before it gets dark."

The day before I'm due to leave, Ann takes me out for a last visit to the hives. The weather is beautiful, the garden full of flowers, and there is much to-ing and fro-ing of the bees.

"I'm glad to see the bees are thriving," I say. "I hope you guys will manage as well. I plan to be back to see you all before too long."

The next morning as I turn onto the highway, I realize the car's enclosed interior is the perfect space for communing with my beloved. Other motorists will simply assume I'm singing along to the radio or that I'm on speakerphone. Often through the journey I talk aloud to Jonah and imagine the words he would use to answer me. Continuing the songlines journey our spirits have been on together and will always be on.

Thirty-Four
September

Once the dean's welcome is over, I join Julie, a girl I know from one of my undergraduate classes. She's heading for the cafeteria.

"Good to see a familiar face," she says. "I'm so glad you made it in—I was way excited when I got my acceptance letter."

"Me too."

I had never expected to be back at university this soon—and at Summerhill, so close to home. I've decided to live at home and commute, at least for the first semester. I don't think Julie knows about Jonah, but who knows? I long ago lost count of all the sympathy emails and Facebook messages I received in the first few weeks after his death.

"Hey, you've got to try these," Julie says as we reach the front of the line. She's holding up a fat package I don't at first recognize. "A kind of jalapeno-cheddar cheese mix. And it's got some added garlic flavouring, I think. Best pretzels you ever tasted, bar none. Whoever thought up that combination?"

I at once remember Ann telling me how she'd sold Jonah's recipe to a company in Ontario. The company had kept Jonah's name for them—Pretzel Mania—and committed to making regular donations to cancer research from the proceeds. I dip my head so Julie doesn't see my lips moving in silent prayer: *I knew you weren't far away, Jonah. Thanks for answering. Just the pick-me-up I needed today.*

The first weeks I spent at home after Jonah's death are a blur. I remember only my tearful departure from Ann and Belinda and Sophie, then my mom telling me there was nothing I had to do but take care of myself. She'd taken leave from her job in the public library just to be home with me. And I'd readily given in to Mom's gentle persuasion after my half-hearted attempts to help around the house. Most days I slept till noon, or later. I skipped breakfast and lunch, made feeble attempts to concentrate on a TV program or a novel, then slept again. Sleep, I came to know, is the most healing power in the cosmos. Then came the day, two or three weeks after I'd arrived home, when I woke early and hungry. I made my way back to my old place at the breakfast table to join my parents.

"I can't stand myself anymore!" I told them. "You were right to send me off to bed when I first got here. But there's only so much sleeping a person can do. I've got to get busy at something."

That day Dad introduced me to Martha, the volunteer director at the community hospital, and I shared some of my story. Martha suggested I work in their mothers' and children's unit as what she called a friendly visitor.

"Your experience at the university with the buddy system makes this a great fit," she told me. "You can help out with the new moms and babies. The nurses will be delighted to have you—they're always run off their feet. Then there's the pediatric ward—you're obviously no stranger to sick children. And most of our patients are short stay anyway, for minor illnesses or operations, so it's a very happy ward. More serious cases get shipped off to the university hospital."

I quickly found caring for others with a thousand small tasks was also healing for me. My energy and humour were still intact, tucked away inside waiting to be unearthed and put to work. The first day I entered the children's ward there were several toddlers running about in street clothes and making a happy hubbub. I introduced myself at the nurses' station, and the charge nurse greeted me with a broad smile.

"We've been expecting you, Ellen. Martha told me you were volunteering. Perfect! I'm Geri—short for Geraldine. We're so glad to have you."

"I'm happy to be here. I'm used to very sick children where I volunteered. Your patients don't look like they're ill at all!"

"Well, these are our new admissions. They're all due for minor surgeries tomorrow—ear tubes, endoscopies, minor plastic procedures. We almost always have empty beds, so we let the parents drop them off the day before, so they don't have to miss work. Pretty much like a baby-sitting service! The parents can be with them again in the evening, and our doctors check them out and write up their pre-ops whenever it suits them."

"Well, put me to work!"

"Great. We like to say our volunteers work for food. Help yourself to anything that's in the kitchen and not labelled for patients only."

After my first day I became a fixture, often finding myself reluctant to head home. Whenever tears welled up, I retreated to the sluice or the washroom till I was ready to show my face again. Geri took me under her wing and I found myself eager to learn how everything ran. Martha had said the nurses were run off their feet, but there was an atmosphere of happy chaos and Geri always had time for me.

"You'd be a natural nurse, you know," she said after my first week. "You see what needs to be done and you never rush anything. Surely you didn't learn bed-making and bed-bathing at Ramsay, did you?"

That was all it took. Geri sat quietly as I told her bits of my story. That I had learned most of my bedside skills from nursing Jonah in his final weeks. All the simple loving skills Sky had taught me. The joy I had felt in caring for Jonah in every way. In playing such a vital part right up to his final breath—and beyond.

"That's the most important word—*caring*," Geri told me. "It's what nursing is at its purest. It comes from *caritas*—Latin for simple love for us human beings." The nurse studied me for a long moment, and I felt familiar tears build. "That's what Mother Teresa brought to every moment of service. Missionaries of Charity she called her communities. And I'm proud to say our profession is leading the way. Medicine has given us countless new therapies—and goes on doing so. But the service, the attention, the loving care—these are the virtues at the core of nursing. And they're as old as humanity. The health care profession is waking up to this once more—because it was never completely lost."

"I never heard it put like that. I met a lot of nurses in the last year after Jonah got sick. They certainly inspired me. Betsy Ormerod, the hospice doctor, told me once she learned everything important from nurses."

"You might have heard about Cicely Saunders, who founded the modern hospice movement in England. She was a nurse, then a social worker, before she ever became a doctor."

"Yes, I've heard of her. Our hospice nurse Sky taught me a whole lot. Where did you do your training, Geri?"

"At Summerhill. It's a great school. There are some advanced thinkers among the professors. They're talking about starting a Centre for Caring, like they have in Colorado and a lot of other places. Why don't you look into it?"

"I think I will. I was set on getting into medical school almost the whole four years of university. But I've pretty much let that go—I don't think it's in my stars to become a doctor."

Geri said no more. When I went over the conversation with my parents, it seemed the nurse had planted a seed. But I quickly realized that seed had been germinating ever since the day I met Beatrix at Dylan's bedside. Then a whole array of nurses since—on the wards, in ICUs and Emergency Rooms. Finally, and most of all, Sky. With her consummate skills in caring for my beloved Jonah, she had taught me the art and science of loving care for people. That seed—Geri had simply brought it to life within me.

"I've never been in doubt," Dad said to me at the dinner table. "Nursing is what health care is founded on. Always has been. I've worked closely with so many wonderful nurses. Doctors may be the ones making all the decisions and ordering all the treatments. But it's the nurses who administer it. They're the ones in closest contact with every patient, night and day."

"Do sleep on it, Ellie," Mom said. "At least for a while before you commit to anything."

"I will, Mom, I will. You know me, I don't jump into things without checking out all the pros and cons. But that's why I have this… this certainty in my mind. In my heart. But I haven't stopped to think what it will take to get into nursing school."

"You've already fulfilled most of the academic requirements for your science degree," Dad said. "And kept up high grades. The nursing school will snap you up!"

"Just take your time deciding, Ellie," my mother repeated.

"I will, Mom. I'll sleep on it, like you said. If I can sleep, that is! I'm so excited!"

Two weeks later I drove to Kingston to interview with the training director in Summerhill's nursing school. I had read and reread the description on the faculty of nursing's website of its flagship Centre for Human Caring, so I felt I could quote its words verbatim: *The Centre promotes and fosters the philosophy and ethics of being in a relationship of deep caring for every human being who comes to us in need.* Grand words, I had thought when

I first read them, but as I went over them, I had come to sense the simple human values they upheld.

"Dr. Ash Graham," she greeted me, coming around her desk to shake my hand. I was at once grateful she didn't stay seated behind her desk for the interview. "I'm delighted you're interested in entering our profession. Thank you for sending your transcripts—you've kept up an exceptional grade average over your three-plus years."

"Thanks. And thank you for seeing me so quickly."

"Well, your situation is unusual. And let me say how sorry I am to hear what happened. I was very moved by the letter you sent me with your transcripts. I'd like to hear a bit more of your experience, if you feel you can share it."

"I'm glad to have the chance to do so," I said. "My few months caring for my husband were a turning point in my life—in more ways than one."

It took me twenty minutes to describe the huge happenings in the eight months between the onset of Jonah's illness and his death. I had rehearsed it as though for a formal interview. This wasn't the time for a sob story. I had to convince Dr. Graham that all my volunteer work with Songlines, the huge learning experience I'd received from countless nurses, and finally my own tending to Jonah alongside Sky and the hospice team, had been one intensive course in caring for others.

Dr. Ash had sat quietly for a long moment when I'd finished. I became aware of the sense of warmth, of safety, that surrounded her. Finally, the training director spoke.

"Ellen, I am proud to meet you, and to hear your words. I'll need to speak to the rest of our admissions committee. But my personal view is that we would welcome you to our nursing program. You might even be able to start classes on Monday next—you'll only have missed the introductory lectures. Then you could be receiving your Bachelor of Science Nursing degree after two years of study—and the world will be open to you."

As she spoke, I felt the certainty growing within me: every act of care I could offer to another would be an offering of love for my beloved Jonah. And an act of healing for myself.

A conversation with Barbara Heatley-O'Neill, R.N., BScN., MAdEd.

John: You're a nurse, coach, and adult educator. What are the primary lessons from this book for you?

Barb: The meaning of the title, "Songlines," as you describe it in the book, resonated with me. Jonah and Ellen journey into the unknown after his diagnosis. Even the physicians acknowledge that the treatment for Jonah's brain cancer is not clearly defined. This in turn means that the prognosis remains agonizingly uncertain until late in the story. That's an important lesson: the unknown features so often in health care.

Second, Ellen refers to "joining the cancer club"—crossing the divide between "them and us." Even though she is not herself afflicted with cancer, she and indeed both families are now part of this club. As a coach I often say that we are always "in choice." But cancer is decidedly not a choice.

Third, I am a great admirer of the role of pharmacists in big hospitals. Pharmacy has come to play such a vital part in every patient's treatment. I'd like to hear a big shout out for our hospital pharmacists.

Fourth, as the story unfolds, Ellen experiences the stages of grief. Most meaningful is when she finally reaches acceptance some months after Jonah's death, and she is now back "in choice." The final sentence was especially moving for me: "Every act of care I can offer to another will be an offering of love for my beloved Jonah. And an act of healing for myself."

John: Dr. MacIsaac praises Jonah for his fighting attitude, saying it can make all the difference, but Ellen has reservations about this. Is it the cancer patient's fault if they don't beat their cancer?

Barb: I never considered that before—that it might well feel like a profound failure if the cancer gets the better of an affected person. So for a caregiver to stress the importance of a fighting attitude could well have the effect of laying a guilt trip on the patient. Very important—we professional caregivers can always encourage the patient to keep a positive attitude, but we must always be right there with our support if things don't go well.

John: When Jonah decides not to take any more anticancer treatment, Dr. MacIsaac reassures him that he isn't giving up, though later Belinda his mom suggests that. What do you think about the notion of "giving up"?

Barb: Absolutely not. It's another example of being "in choice." Jonah shows a special kind of courage in deciding to take charge of his life and of his cancer treatment. And I was glad the oncologist clearly supported him.

Another thing: the hospice nurse, Sky, tells Ellen that many people die at night. That is absolutely my experience. You put it in context with the hospice nurse's words—"It's almost as if they take their loved ones' sleeping as permission to enter their own eternal slumber."

John: Why do you think books about health, and particularly about dying—fiction or nonfiction—are so popular?

Barb: I think it's because of our human condition. We are all curious because we know we're going to be there one day—it's part of the human story.

John: What about Ellen proposing marriage to Jonah once they both know what's ahead for them both? Any thoughts?

Barb: Yes, that did surprise me at first. Then I realized that they were simply marking the traditional stages of life. This young couple are deeply in love and committed to each other, and they want to mark this commitment, for however long they have together. And also, it gave both Jonah's and Ellen's family and Jonah's and Ellen's friends a focus and a way of relating to each other at such a hard, hard time.

John: Any thoughts about the sex scenes, or about the inclusion of a same-sex marriage?

Barb: I liked both these inclusions. Very refreshing and contemporary. It would be helpful especially for a young man with cancer to know that his sex life could continue, despite the initial difficulties you describe. And having two moms—Jonah describes it in a very low-key way, not making a big deal of it. I liked that a lot.

John: Have you had experience with art and music in hospitals?

Barb: Oh yes. Not long ago in Windsor, Ontario, I was with a colleague waiting for a meeting and suddenly these clowns appeared and "serenaded" us for a few minutes. It was a lovely diversion and kind of reset the clock, so that we no longer felt we had been waiting forever for our meeting. And I was at a conference run by Patch Adams, called "Joy: The Forgotten Vital Sign." A lot of art—it was wonderful.

I loved the music in your book—especially the choices. I downloaded some of them and found them refreshing and lovely. And I loved the idea of a professional actor teaching the students bedside skills. Beautiful.

John: Yes, art of all kinds is finding more and more of a role in hospitals. There's a lot of evidence that music played at the bedside of the dying can be soothing and uplifting.

Did you find the role of the palliative care team appropriate to Jonah's and the family's care?

Barb: Very much so. I remember when the mention of palliative care was seen as an absolute death knell—that it meant the patient would die that very day. I'm glad to say this is changing in many places. I remember when I was head nurse at Sarnia and we created palliative care "orders" for every unit. The nurses all got it, though I'm sorry to say the doctors still had a hard time with the idea, thinking of themselves as having failed in their job. But actually many, perhaps most, illnesses today are incurable, so palliative care plays a crucial role, and not just when a patient is about to die.

John: I'm very glad to hear you say that. When I became a hospice and palliative care director, I spent a lot of time trying to convince my faculty colleagues and the resident doctors that it wasn't a matter of *either/or* but of *both/and*. That one could still be bent on ultimately curing a patient but that palliative care can often, if not always, still play a role.

Barb: Yes. It's about "being" and "doing." Professional caregivers often have the mindset that they must be actively *doing* something to or for the patient, but in fact just *being* with him or her is of vital importance too. It's about compassion, deep listening, witnessing, holding the space. I love the acronym, "WAIT" used in palliative care, meaning "Why Am I Talking?" Why don't I just shut up and listen!

John: Any last thoughts?

Barb: Well, I loved the caring philosophy that ran throughout the book. A vital message to readers. This book would be ideal for a book club reading, with our discussion serving as a prompt.

Dear Kim:

I hope you hear conversations that you and I have shared, in the words here, you and I have journeyed together through so many events!

I hope that you enjoy the book as much as I did.

Love

Barb.

Acknowledgments

To my dear friend and colleague, Rebecca Brown, founder of *Street-light*, a palliative care program for the psychosocial needs of adolescents and young adults living with life-limiting illnesses. And to the hundreds of college students at the University of Florida who have loved and befriended these young people through their "valley of the shadow of death."

To the friends and colleagues too numerous to mention who have helped me with this book, and with my "second career" as a writer. Most especial thanks to Marianne Ward for her immeasurably wise editorial advice.

As a community-based cooperative, HARP The People's Press (www.harppublishing.ca) works with many local artists. I offer a special thanks to Gillian McCulloch for the cover art, to Cathy Lin for the layout and design, and to Denise Davies for her promotion and countless other tasks.

Last and most enduring, my love and gratitude to the multitude of young people and their families whom I've been privileged to serve over close to half a century.

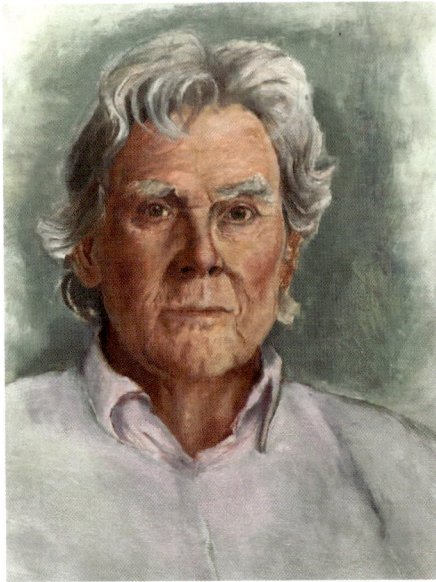

John Graham-Pole is a retired professor of pediatrics. He has been a clinician, teacher and pioneer researcher in the field of childhood cancer for forty years. Educated in the United Kingdom, he co-founded the Center for Arts in Medicine (www.arts.ufl.edu) at the University of Florida, now among the world's leading arts-and-health organizations.

He is the author of many works of non-fiction, fiction, and poetry. He lives in Nova Scotia with his wife, Dorothy Lander, where they co-founded HARP The People's Press (www.harppublishing.ca), which is dedicated to producing print and online publications on art and health for a diverse readership. *Songlines* is the third of a trilogy of novels inspired by children and young adults with cancer.

John's personal website is www.johngrahampole.com, and he shares the HARP website with his wife and co-publisher. He can also be found on Facebook, Instagram, and Linked In.

The two earlier books in the *Heroes* trilogy—also novels inspired by young people with cancer—are available directly from HARP: The People's Press (www.harppublishing.ca), or from major distribution outlets. These are shown on the following page.

The Circle of Abundance Indigenous Program, Coady International Institute, St. Francis Xavier University: https://coady.stfx.ca/circle-of-abundance;and David Suzuki Foundation (one nature): https://davidsuzuki.org receive 20% of all sales, distributed equally.

Life-and-death adventure, coming-of-age romance, and true-to-life account of 16-year-old Raig Broussard's battle with cancer. A fictional follow-up to John Graham-Pole's medical memoir, *Journeys With 1000 Heroes: A Child Oncologist's Story*

"A beautifully written story that will capture the hearts and imagination of all readers" - Sheldon Currie

CAN $20.99/US $15.99

Blood Work
John Graham-Pole

A true-to-life-and-death story of 11-year-old Jeremy's journey with leukemia. The second of the author's trilogy of novels about heroic young people with cancer, following on Blood Work, published by HARP in 2019

'Tears of sorrow, laughter and joy heal us as our souls connect with this boy who found his own soul' - Sandra Bertman

ISBN 9780993829550

A Boy and His Soul
John Graham-Pole